THE MUDFOG PAPERS

CHARLES DICKENS

THE MUDFOG PAPERS

ALAN SUTTON
1987

Alan Sutton Publishing Limited
Brunswick Road · Gloucester

First published 1880

Copyright © in this edition 1984
Alan Sutton Publishing Limited

Reprinted 1987

British Library Cataloguing in Publication Data

Dickens, Charles, *1812–1870*
 The Mudfog papers.
 I. Title
 823′.8[F]   PR4572.M7/

 ISBN 0-86299-151-X

*Cover picture: detail from an engraving by John Leech;
hand tinted by Shelagh Davies*

Typesetting and origination by
Alan Sutton Publishing Limited
Photoset Bembo 9/10
Printed in Great Britain
by The Guernsey Press Company Limited
Guernsey, Channel Islands.

BIOGRAPHICAL NOTE

CHARLES DICKENS (1812–1870). A man of singular imagination, novelist, editor, journalist, theatrical producer, actor and a supporter of radical reform, Charles Dickens was one of the great Victorians. He was born in Portsmouth on 7 February 1812, the second child of John, a clerk in the Navy Pay Office, and Elizabeth, who were extroverts and continually living beyond their sufficient but modest means, apparently more interested in themselves than in their children. He spent a happy early childhood in Portsmouth, London and Chatham, entertained by the macabre stories of his nursemaid, and later by his own wide reading, and developing imagination. In 1822 John Dickens was reposted to London, and his financial situation, already perilous, quickly went from bad to worse. Charles was unable to attend school, and two years later was sent to work in a boot-blacking factory, where he met with some of the rougher elements of London life. Meanwhile his father was declared bankrupt, and escorted with his family to the Marshalsea, while Charles had lodgings near his work, and visited the prison frequently. Fortunately, this sad state of affairs lasted only a few months, and later in the year, at the age of twelve, Charles was sent back to school to complete his education. He left school at fifteen, and by the age of twenty-three had established himself as a journalist and man of the theatre.

Four years later he was a first ranking man of letters, a husband and a father. He had written the first of the *Sketches by Boz* in 1833, and, in 1836, *Pickwick* started to appear in serial form, to be followed by *Oliver Twist* (1838) and *Nicholas Nickleby* (1839). Dickens had become editor of *Bentley's Miscellany*, in which the first parts of *Mudfog* were published in 1837, and was receiving a steady income. He had married Catherine Hogarth in 1836, and had been devasted by the death, one year later, of Mary, his sister-in-law, whom he loved dearly. By 1839 he was able to move his impecunious parents to Devon, and buy a family house in London. His writings were based on his own experiences and concerns: childhood problems and poverty pervade *Oliver Twist*; ideas of education and the theatre appear in *Nicholas Nickleby*; while in *The Old Curiosity Shop* (1841), he invokes memories of the beloved Mary, and *Barnaby Rudge* (also 1841) reflects Dickens' visits to Newgate Prison, his intimate knowledge of the London underworld and his political sympathies.

Dickens' experiences were broadened in 1842, when he made a triumphant visit to America. Although he was warmly welcomed, he did not like America, and was profoundly affected by his encounters with slavery and a visit to a penal institute practising solitary confinement. His criticism of American society was lightly veiled in the ensuing *American Notes* (1842), and continued in *Martin Chuzzlewit* (1844), another study of a disturbed childhood, which included a journey to the States. Dickens' support for radical reformers in England developed with his reputation, and he was frequently a public speaker for charitable institutions. He was particularly concerned with the plight of children, and was inspired to write *Christmas Carol* (1843) by a visit to Miss Angela Burdett Coutts' Ragged School for deprived Cockney children, in order 'to present the poor in a favourable light to the rich.'

In 1844, after ten years of intensive work, Dickens took his family to Italy for a year's break. The family included five children and Georgina, Catherine's younger sister, who had lived with the family since 1842. Not unnaturally for a man of his temperament, Dickens missed London and his many friends, but was stimulated by an experiment in mesmerism with Madame de la Rue, an attractive English woman who suffered from hallucinations. This relationship and the foreign environment exacerbated the relationship between Dickens and his wife, and marked the beginning of their final estrangement.

The next six years (1845–51) were busy ones. Besides spending nine months travelling and writing in Switzerland and Paris, Dickens was working as actor-manager of an amateur dramatic group, performing in London and touring the provinces. He was involved in an abortive attempt to establish a radical newspaper, but finally, in 1850, achieved his dream of producing his own journal, *Household Words*, which was an instant success, and employed many of Dickens' friends, his father and his father-in-law. Its purpose was to generate social awareness and press for social reform. Two years earlier Dickens had opened Urania Cottage, a home for reclaimed prostitutes, under the patronage of Angela Coutts, and he retained responsibility for it as an unpaid superinten-dent. During these years he worked on *Dombey and Son* (1848), a study in selfishness, and *David Copperfield* (1850), a semi-autobiographical novel, which explored once more Dickens' own unsatisfactory childhood. In 1851 a series of misfortunes afflicted the Dickens' household. After the birth of their ninth child, Catherine suffered a nervous breakdown and was taken to Malvern for treatment. While she was away, first Charles' father, and then this last child died. Restlessness and concern for Catherine's well-being induced Dickens to move the family to a new home in Tavistock Square, while ideas of a new book whirled through his mind.

Bleak House (1853), was completed when Dickens was forty-one, and the end of that year saw Dickens give the first of his famous public readings of his own work. But the years of frenzied activity had taken their toll, and during that same year Dickens had been forced to take holidays in Europe, to avoid a nervous breakdown. Although he escaped a break-down, Dickens continued to be possessed by a restlessness and feverish energy which he never lost, in spite of taking regular working holidays in Folkestone and France. *Bleak House* is a vast rambling criticism of the British legal system, and, like it, his two subsequent novels were satirical comments on Victo-rian 'systems'. *Hard Times* (1854), comments on the effects of mechanization on society and education, while in *Little Dorrit* (1857), Dickens explored the way in which people are im-prisoned in their social milieu. Little Dorrit herself was modelled on Georgina Hogarth, who had lived with the family for the last fourteen years, a companion to Catherine, nanny to the ten children and beloved 'sister' of Charles. In 1857 Dickens, still involved in theatricals, took a production of Wilkie Collins' melodrama *The Frozen Deep* to Manchester, and invited the actress Mrs Ternan and two of her daughters to take the female parts.

Ellen Ternan, the younger daughter, was an attractive eighteen-year-old. Dickens fell in love with her, and within the year, inspite of criticism from his friends, colleagues and readers had separated from Catherine, who moved out of Tavistock House. Since he now had three households to maintain, Tavistock House, Gad's Hill, which he had purchased as a country residence in 1857, and Mrs Dickens' new home in Gloucester Crescent, as well as the Ternans to support, Dickens needed to supplement his income, and this he did by making extensive tours to give public readings in England, Scotland and Ireland. At the same time, he continued his work as editor and journalist for *Household Words* until, through ill feeling, he changed publishers, and started producing a new journal called *All the Year Round*. The publication of the new magazine stimulated the writing of the next two serial novels: *A Tale of Two Cities* (1859), to establish a wide readership, and *Great Expectations* (1861) to maintain it. The first explored themes of death and resurrection against the violence of the French Revolution, while the second returned to thoughts of childhood and adolescent love in a plot involving mistaken identity. It also contained many shorter stories including 'The Signalman' (1866).

In 1860, Dickens sold Tavistock House, and the next few years were spent at Gad's Hill, or in London or Paris, giving regular readings and writing *Our Mutual Friend* (1865), a study of material greed and mistaken identity. He also paid regular visits to Ellen, who was now living in Slough. The years were beginning to tell, and although he was now a wealthy man, he continued to press himself beyond the limit. In 1865, he suffered the first of regular bouts of trouble with his feet, as well as being badly shaken in a rail accident. However, in 1867, at the age of fifty-five, he set out for a victorious five month reading tour of the States, returning to a hero's welcome. But his final tour of the English provinces was not completed because of ill health, and in January 1870, he gave his last readings in London. He died on 9 June 1870 of a cerebral haemorrhage, leaving his final novel, *Edwin Drood*, unfinished. He was buried in Poets' Corner, Westminster Abbey.

SHEILA MICHELL

PUBLIC LIFE OF MR. TULRUMBLE
ONCE MAYOR OF MUDFOG

Mudfog is a pleasant town – a remarkably pleasant town – situated in a charming hollow by the side of a river, from which river, Mudfog derives an agreeable scent of pitch, tar, coals, and rope-yarn, a roving population in oil-skin hats, a pretty steady influx of drunken bargemen, and a great many other maritime advantages. There is a good deal of water about Mudfog, and yet it is not exactly the sort of town for a watering-place, either. Water is a perverse sort of element at the best of times, and in Mudfog it is particularly so. In winter, it comes oozing down the streets and tumbling over the fields, – nay, rushes into the very cellars and kitchens of the houses, with a lavish prodigality that might well be dispensed with; but in the hot summer weather it *will* dry up, and turn green: and, although green is a very good colour in its way, especially in grass, still it certainly is not becoming to water; and it cannot be denied that the beauty of Mudfog is rather impaired, even by this trifling circumstance. Mudfog is a healthy place – very healthy; – damp, perhaps, but none the worse for that. It's quite a mistake to suppose that damp is unwholesome: plants thrive best in damp situations, and why shouldn't men? The inhabitants of Mudfog are unanimous in asserting that there exists not a finer race of people on the face of the earth; here we have an indisputable and veracious contradiction of the vulgar error at once. So, admitting Mudfog to be damp, we distinctly state that it is salubrious.

The town of Mudfog is extremely picturesque. Limehouse and Ratcliff Highway are both something like it, but they give you a very faint idea of Mudfog. There are a great many more public-houses in Mudfog – more than in Ratcliff Highway and Limehouse put together. The public buildings, too, are very imposing. We consider the town-hall one of the finest specimens of shed architecture, extant: it is a combination of the pig-sty and tea-garden-box, orders; and the simplicity of its design is of surpassing beauty. The idea of placing a large window on one side of the door, and a small one on the other, is particularly happy. There is a fine bold Doric beauty, too, about the padlock and scraper, which is strictly in keeping with the general effect.

In this room do the mayor and corporation of Mudfog assemble together in solemn council for the public weal. Seated on the massive wooden benches, which, with the table in the centre, form the only furniture of the whitewashed apartment, the sage men of Mudfog spend hour after hour in grave deliberation. Here they settle at what hour of the night the public-houses shall be closed, at what hour of the morning they shall be permitted to open, how soon it shall be lawful for people to eat their dinner on church-days, and other great political questions; and sometimes, long after silence has fallen on the town, and the distant lights from the shops and houses have ceased to twinkle, like far-off stars, to the sight of the boatmen on the river, the illumination in the two unequal-sized windows of the town-hall, warns the inhabitants of Mudfog that its little body of legislators, like a larger and better-known body of the same genus, a great deal more noisy, and not a whit more profound, are patriotically dozing away in company, far into the night, for their country's good.

Among this knot of sage and learned men, no one was so eminently distinguished, during many years, for the quiet modesty of his appearance and demeanour, as Nicholas Tulrumble, the well-known coal-dealer. However exciting the subject of discussion, however animated the tone of the debate, or however warm the personalities exchanged, (and even in Mudfog we get personal sometimes,) Nicholas Tulrumble was always the same. To say truth, Nicholas, being an industrious man, and always up betimes, was apt to fall asleep when a debate began, and to remain asleep till it was over, when he would wake up very much refreshed, and give his vote with the greatest complacency. The fact was, that Nicholas Tulrumble, knowing that everybody there had made up his mind beforehand, considered the talking as just a long botheration about nothing at all; and to the present hour it remains a question, whether, on this point at all events, Nicholas Tulrumble was not pretty near right.

Time, which strews a man's head with silver, sometimes fills his pockets with gold. As he gradually performed one good office for Nicholas Tulrumble, he was obliging enough, not to omit the other. Nicholas began life in a wooden tenement of four feet square, with a capital of two and ninepence, and a stock in trade of three bushels and a half of coals, exclusive of the large lump which hung, by way of a sign-board, outside. Then he enlarged the shed, and kept a truck; then he left the shed, and the truck too, and started a donkey and a Mrs. Tulrumble; then he moved again and set up a cart; the cart was soon afterwards exchanged for a waggon; and so he went on like his great predecessor Whittington — only without a cat for a partner — increasing in wealth and fame, until at last he gave up business altogether, and retired with Mrs. Tulrumble and family to Mudfog Hall, which he had himself erected, on something which he attempted to delude himself into the belief was a hill, about a quarter of a mile distant from the town of Mudfog.

About this time, it began to be murmured in Mudfog that Nicholas Tulrumble was growing vain and haughty; that prosperity and success had corrupted the simplicity of his manners, and tainted the natural goodness of his heart; in short, that he was setting up for a public character, and a great gentleman, and affected to look down upon his old companions with compassion and contempt. Whether these reports were at the time well-founded, or not, certain it is that Mrs. Tulrumble very shortly afterwards started a four-wheel chaise, driven by a tall postilion in a yellow cap, – that Mr. Tulrumble junior took to smoking cigars, and calling the footman a 'feller,' – and that Mr. Tulrumble from that time forth, was no more seen in his old seat in the chimney-corner of the Lighterman's Arms at night. This looked bad; but, more than this, it began to be observed that Mr. Nicholas Tulrumble attended the corporation meetings more frequently than heretofore; and he no longer went to sleep as he had done for so many years, but propped his eyelids open with his two fore-fingers; that he read the newspapers by himself at home; and that he was in the habit of indulging abroad in distant and mysterious allusions to 'masses of people,' and 'the property of the country,' and 'productive power,' and 'the monied interest:' all of which denoted and proved that Nicholas Tulrumble was either mad, or worse; and it puzzled the good people of Mudfog amazingly.

At length, about the middle of the month of October, Mr. Tulrumble and family went up to London; the middle of October being, as Mrs. Tulrumble informed her acquaintance in Mudfog, the very height of the fashionable season.

Somehow or other, just about this time, despite the health-preserving air of Mudfog, the Mayor died. It was a most extraordinary circumstance; he had lived in Mudfog for eighty-five years. The corporation didn't understand it at all; indeed it was with great difficulty that one old gentleman, who was a great stickler for forms, was dissuaded from proposing a vote of censure on such unaccountable conduct. Strange as it was, however, die he did, without taking the slightest notice of the corporation; and the corporation were imperatively called upon to elect his successor. So, they met for the purpose; and being very full of Nicholas Tulrumble just then, and Nicholas Tulrumble being a very important man, they elected him, and wrote off to London by the very next post to acquaint Nicholas Tulrumble with his new elevation.

Now, it being November time, and Mr. Nicholas Tulrumble being in the capital, it fell out that he was present at the Lord Mayor's show and dinner, at sight of the glory and splendour whereof, he, Mr. Tulrumble, was greatly mortified, inasmuch as the reflection would force itself on his mind, that, had he been born in London instead of in Mudfog, he might have been a Lord Mayor too, and have patronized the judges, and been affable to the Lord Chancellor, and friendly with the Premier, and coldly condescending to the Secretary to the Treasury, and have dined with a flag behind his back, and done a great many other acts and deeds which unto Lord Mayors of London peculiarly appertain. The more he thought of the Lord Mayor, the more enviable a personage he seemed. To be a King was all very well; but what was the King to the Lord Mayor! When the King made a speech, everybody knew it was somebody else's writing; whereas here was the Lord Mayor, talking away for half an hour – all out of his own head – admidst the enthusiastic applause of the whole company, while it was notorious that the King might talk to his parliament till he was black in the face without getting so much as a single cheer. As all these reflections passed through the mind of Mr. Nicholas Tulrumble, the Lord Mayor of London appeared to him the greatest sovereign on the face of the earth, beating the Emperor of Russia all to nothing, and leaving the Great Mogul immeasurably behind.

Mr. Nicholas Tulrumble was pondering over these things, and inwardly cursing the fate which had pitched his coal-shed in Mudfog, when the letter of the corporation was put into his hand. A crimson flush mantled over his face as he read it, for visions of brightness were already dancing before his imagination.

'My dear,' said Mr. Tulrumble to his wife, 'they have elected me, Mayor of Mudfog.'

'Lor-a-mussy!' said Mrs. Tulrumble: 'why what's become of old Sniggs?'

'The late Mr. Sniggs, Mrs. Tulrumble,' said Mr. Tulrumble sharply, for he by no means approved of the notion of unceremoniously designating a gentleman who filled the high office of Mayor, as 'Old Sniggs,' – 'The late Mr. Sniggs, Mrs. Tulrumble, is dead.'

The communication was very unexpected; but Mrs. Tulrumble only ejaculated 'Lor-a-mussy!' once again, as if a Mayor were a mere ordinary Christian, at which Mr. Tulrumble frowned gloomily.

'What a pity 'tan't in London, ain't it?' said Mrs. Tulrumble, after a short pause; 'what a pity 'tan't in London, where you might have had a show.'

'I *might* have a show in Mudfog, if I thought proper, I apprehend,' said Mr. Tulrumble mysteriously.

'Lor! so you might, I declare,' replied Mrs. Tulrumble.

'And a good one too,' said Mr. Tulrumble.

'Delightful!' exclaimed Mrs. Tulrumble.

'One which would rather astonish the ignorant people down there,' said Mr. Tulrumble.

'It would kill them with envy,' said Mrs. Tulrumble.

So it was agreed that his Majesty's lieges in Mudfog should be astonished with splendour, and slaughtered with envy, and that such a show should take place as had never been seen in that town, or in any other town before, – no, not even in London itself.

On the very next day after the receipt of the letter, down came the tall postilion in a post-chaise, – not upon one of the horses, but inside – actually inside the chaise, – and, driving up to the very door of the town-hall, where the corporation were assembled, delivered a letter, written by the Lord knows who, and signed by Nicholas Tulrumble, in which Nicholas said, all through four sides of closely-written, gilt-edged, hot-pressed, Bath post letter paper, that he responded to the call of his fellow-townsmen with feelings of heartfelt delight; that he accepted the arduous office which their confidence had imposed upon him; that they would never find him shrinking from the discharge of his duty; that he would endeavour to execute his functions with all that dignity which their magnitude and importance demanded; and a great more to the same effect. But even this was not all. The tall postilion produced from his right-hand top-boot, a damp copy of that afternoon's number of the county paper; and there, in large type, running the whole length of the very first column, was a long address from Nicholas Tulrumble to the inhabitants of Mudfog, in which he said that he cheerfully complied with their requisition, and, in short, as if to prevent any mistake about the matter, told them over again what a grand fellow he meant to be, in very much the same terms as those in which he had already told them all about the matter in his letter.

The corporation stared at one another very hard at all this, and then looked as if for explanation to the tall postilion, but as the tall postilion was intently contemplating the gold tassel on the top of his yellow cap, and could have afforded no explanation whatever, even if his thoughts had been entirely disengaged, they contented themselves with coughing very dubiously, and looking very grave. The tall postilion then delivered another letter, in which Nicholas Tulrumble informed the corporation, that he intended repairing to the town-hall, in grand state and gorgeous procession, on the Monday afternoon next ensuing. At this the corporation looked still more solemn; but, as the epistle wound up with a formal invitation to the whole body to dine with the Mayor on that day, at Mudfog Hall, Mudfog Hill, Mudfog, they began to see the fun of the thing directly, and sent back their compliments, and they'd be sure to come.

Now there happened to be in Mudfog, as somehow or other there does happen to be, in almost every town in the British dominions, and perhaps in foreign dominions too – we think it very likely, but, being no great traveller, cannot distinctly say – there happened to be, in Mudfog, a merry-tempered, pleasant-faced, good-for-nothing sort of vagabond, with an invincible dislike to manual labour, and an unconquerable attachment to strong beer and spirits, whom everybody knew, and nobody, except his wife, took the trouble to quarrel with, who inherited from his ancestors the appellation of Edward Twigger, and rejoiced in the *sobriquet* of Bottle-nosed Ned. He was drunk upon the average once a day, and penitent upon an equally fair calculation once a month; and when he was penitent, he was invariably in the very last stage of maudlin intoxication. He was a ragged, roving, roaring kind of fellow, with a burly form, a sharp wit, and a ready head, and could turn his hand to anything when he chose to do it. He was by no means opposed to hard labour on principle, for he would work away at a cricket-match by the day together, – running, and catching, and batting, and bowling, and revelling in toil which would exhaust a galley-slave. He would have been invaluable to a fire-office; never was a man with such a natural taste for pumping engines, running up ladders, and throwing furniture out of two-pair-of-stairs' windows: nor was this the only element in which he was at home; he was a humane society in himself, a portable drag, an animated life-preserver, and had saved more people, in his time, from drowning, than the Plymouth life-boat, or Captain Manby's apparatus. With all these qualifications, notwithstanding his dissipation, Bottle-nosed Ned was a general favourite; and the authorities of Mudfog, remembering his numerous services to the popula-tion, allowed him in return to get drunk in his own way, without the fear of stocks, fine, or imprisonment. He had a general licence, and he showed his sense of the compliment by making the most of it.

We have been thus particular in describing the character and avocations of Bottle-nosed Ned, because it enables us to introduce a fact politely, without hauling it into the reader's presence with indecent haste by the head and shoulders, and brings us very naturally to relate, that on the very same evening on which Mr. Nicholas Tulrumble and family returned to Mudfog, Mr. Tulrumble's new secretary, just imported from London, with a pale face and light whiskers, thrust his head down to the very bottom of his neckcloth-tie, in at the tap-room door of the Lighterman's Arms, and inquiring whether one Ned Twigger was luxuriating within, announced himself as the bearer of a message from Nicholas Tulrumble, Esquire, requiring Mr. Twigger's immediate attendance at the hall, on private and particular business. It being by no means Mr. Twigger's interest to affront the Mayor, he rose from the fire-place with a slight sigh, and followed the light-whiskered secretary through the dirt and wet of Mudfog streets, up to Mudfog Hall, without further ado.

Mr. Nicholas Tulrumble was seated in a small cavern with a skylight, which he called his library, sketching out a plan of the procession on a large sheet of paper; and into the cavern the secretary ushered Ned Twigger.

'Well, Twigger!' said Nicholas Tulrumble, condescendingly.

There was a time when Twigger would have replied, 'Well, Nick!' but that was in the days of the truck, and a couple of years before the donkey; so, he only bowed.

'I want you to go into training, Twigger,' said Mr. Tulrumble.

'What for, sir?' inquired Ned, with a stare.

'Hush, hush, Twigger!' said the Mayor. 'Shut the door, Mr. Jennings. Look here, Twigger.'

As the Mayor said this, he unlocked a high closet, and disclosed a complete suit of brass armour, of gigantic dimensions.

'I want you to wear this next Monday, Twigger,' said the Mayor.

'Bless your heart and soul, sir!' replied Ned, 'you might as well ask me to wear a seventy-four pounder, or a cast-iron boiler.'

'Nonsense, Twigger, nonsense!' said the Mayor.

'I couldn't stand under it, sir,' said Twigger; 'it would make mashed potatoes of me, if I attempted it.'

'Pooh, pooh, Twigger!' returned the Mayor. 'I tell you I have seen it done with my own eyes, in London, and the man wasn't half such a man as you are, either.'

'I should as soon have thought of a man's wearing the case of an eight-day clock to save his linen,' said Twigger, casting a look of apprehension at the brass suit.

'It's the easiest thing in the world,' rejoined the Mayor.

'It's nothing,' said Mr. Jennings.

'When you're used to it,' added Ned.

'You do it by degrees,' said the Mayor. 'You would begin with one piece tomorrow, and two the next day, and so on, till you had got it all on. Mr. Jennings, give Twigger a glass of rum. Just try the breast-plate, Twigger. Stay; take another glass of rum first. Help me to lift it, Mr. Jennings. Stand firm, Twigger! There! – it isn't half as heavy as it looks, is it?'

Twigger was a good strong, stout fellow; so, after a great deal of staggering, he managed to keep himself up, under the breast-plate, and even contrived, with the aid of another glass of rum, to walk about in it, and the gauntlets into the bargain. He made a trial of the helmet, but was not equally successful, inasmuch as he tipped over instantly, – an accident which Mr. Tulrumble clearly demonstrated to be occasioned by his not having a counteracting weight of brass on his legs.

'Now, wear that with grace and propriety on Monday next,' said Tulrumble, 'and I'll make your fortune.'

'I'll try what I can do, sir,' said Twigger.

'It must be kept a profound secret,' said Tulrumble.

'Of course, sir,' replied Twigger.

'And you must be sober,' said Tulrumble; 'perfectly sober.'

Mr. Twigger at once solemnly pledged himself to be as sober as a judge, and Nicholas Tulrumble was satisfied, although, had we been Nicholas, we should certainly have exacted some promise of a more specific nature; inasmuch as, having attended the Mudfog assizes in the evening more than once, we can solemnly testify to having seen judges with very strong symptoms of dinner under their wigs. However, that's neither here nor there.

The next day, and the day following, and the day after that, Ned Twigger was securely locked up in the small cavern with the skylight, hard at work at the armour. With every additional piece he could manage to stand upright in, he had an additional glass of rum; and at last, after many partial suffocations, he contrived to get on the whole suit, and to stagger up and down the room in it, like an intoxicated effigy from Westminster Abbey.

Never was man so delighted as Nicholas Tulrumble; never was woman so charmed as Nicholas Tulrumble's wife. Here was a sight for the common people of Mudfog! A live man in brass armour! Why, they would go wild with wonder!

The day – *the* Monday – arrived.

If the morning had been made to order, it couldn't have been better adapted to the purpose. They never showed a better fog in London on Lord Mayor's day, than enwrapped the town of Mudfog on that eventful occasion. It had risen slowly and surely from the green and stagnant water with the first light of morning, until it reached a little above the lamp-post tops; and there it had stopped, with a sleepy, sluggish obstinacy, which bade defiance to the sun, who had got up very blood-shot about the eyes, as if he had been at a drinking-party over night, and was doing his day's work with the worst possible grace. The thick damp mist hung over the town like a huge gauze curtain. All was dim and dismal. The church steeples had bidden a temporary adieu to the world below; and every object of lesser importance – houses, barns, hedges, trees, and barges – had all taken the veil.

The church-clock struck one. A cracked trumpet from the front garden of Mudfog Hall produced a feeble flourish, as if some asthmatic person had coughed into it accidentally; the gate flew open, and out came a gentleman, on a moist-sugar coloured charger, intended to represent a herald, but bearing a much stronger resemblance to a court-card on horseback. This was one of the Circus people, who always came down to Mudfog at that time of the year, and who had been engaged by Nicholas Tulrumble expressly for the occasion. There was the horse, whisking his tail about, balancing himself on his hind-legs, and flourishing away with his fore-feet, in a manner which would have gone to the hearts and souls of any reasonable crowd. But a Mudfog crowd never was a reasonable one, and in all probability never will be. Instead of scattering the very fog with their shouts, as they ought most indubitably to have done, and were fully intended to do, by Nicholas Tulrumble, they no sooner recognized the herald, than they began to growl forth the most unqualified disapprobation at the bare notion of his riding like any other man. If he had come out on his head indeed, or jumping through a hoop, or flying through a red-hot drum, or even standing on one leg with his other foot in his mouth, they might have had something to say to him; but for a professional gentleman to sit astride in the saddle, with his feet in the stirrups, was rather too good a joke. So, the herald was a decided failure, and the crowd hooted with great energy, as he pranced ingloriously away.

On the procession came. We are afraid to say how many supernumeraries there were, in striped shirts and black velvet caps, to imitate the London watermen, or how many base imitations of running-footmen, or how many banners, which, owing to the heaviness of the atmosphere, could by no means be prevailed on to display their inscriptions: still less do we feel disposed to relate how the men who played the wind instruments, looking up into the sky (we mean the fog) with musical fervour, walked through pools of water and hillocks of mud, till they covered the powdered heads of the running-footmen aforesaid with splashes, that looked curious, but not ornamental; or how the barrel-organ performer put on the wrong stop, and played one tune while the band played another; or how the horses, being used to the arena, and not to the streets, would stand still and dance, instead of going on and prancing; – all of which are matters which might be dilated upon to great advantage, but which we have not the least intention of dilating upon, notwithstanding.

Oh! it was a grand and beautiful sight to behold a corporation in glass coaches, provided at the sole cost and charge of Nicholas Tulrumble, coming rolling along, like a funeral out of mourning, and to watch the attempts the corporation made to look great and solemn, when Nicholas Tulrumble himself, in the four-wheel chaise, with the tall postilion, rolled out after them, with Mr. Jennings on one side to look like a chaplain, and a supernumerary on the other, with an old life-guardsman's sabre, to imitate the sword-bearer; and to see the tears rolling down the faces of the mob as they screamed with merriment. This was beautiful! and so was the appearance of Mrs. Tulrumble and son, as they bowed with grave dignity out of their coach-window to all the dirty faces that were laughing around them: but it is not even with this that we have to do, but with the sudden stopping of the procession at another blast of the trumpet, whereat, and whereupon, a profound silence ensued, and all eyes were turned towards Mudfog Hall, in the confidant anticipation of some new wonder.

'They won't laugh now, Mr. Jennings,' said Nicholas Tulrumble.

'I think not, sir,' said Mr. Jennings.

'See how eager they look,' said Nicholas Tulrumble. 'Aha! the laugh will be on our side now; eh, Mr. Jennings?'

'No doubt of that, sir,' replied Mr. Jennings; and Nicholas Tulrumble, in a state of pleasurable excitement, stood up in the four-wheel chaise, and telegraphed gratification to the Mayoress behind.

While all this was going forward, Ned Twigger had descended into the kitchen of Mudfog Hall for the purpose of indulging the servants with a private view of the curiosity that was to burst upon the town; and, somehow or other, the footman was so companionable, and the housemaid so kind, and the cook so friendly, that he could not resist the offer of the first-mentioned to sit down and take something – just to drink success to master in.

So, down Ned Twigger sat himself in his brass livery on the top of the kitchen-table; and in a mug of something strong, paid for by the unconscious Nicholas Tulrumble, and provided by the companionable footman, drank success to the Mayor and his procession; and, as Ned laid by his helmet to imbibe the something strong, the companionable footman put it on his own head, to the immeasurable and unrecordable delight of the cook and housemaid. The companionable footman was very facetious to Ned, and Ned was very gallant to the cook and housemaid by turns. They were all very cosy and comfortable; and the something strong went briskly round.

At last Ned Twigger was loudly called for, by the procession people: and, having had his helmet fixed on, in a very complicated manner, by the companionable footman, and the kind housemaid, and the friendly cook, he walked gravely forth, and appeared before the multitude.

The crowd roared – it was not with wonder, it was not with surprise; it was most decidedly and unquestionably with laughter.

'What!' said Mr. Tulrumble, starting up in the four-wheel chaise. 'Laughing? If they laugh at a man in real brass armour, they'd laugh when their own fathers were dying. Why doesn't he go into his place, Mr. Jennings? What's he rolling down towards us for? he has no business here!'

'I am afraid, sir——' faltered Mr. Jennings.

'Afraid of what, sir?' said Nicholas Tulrumble, looking up into the secretary's face.

'I am afraid he's drunk, sir,' replied Mr. Jennings.

Nicholas Tulrumble took one look at the extraordinary figure that was bearing down upon them; and then, clasping his secretary by the arm, uttered an audible groan in anguish of spirit.

It is a melancholy fact that Mr. Twigger having full licence to demand a single glass of rum on the putting on of every piece of the armour, got, by some means or other, rather out of his calculation in the hurry and confusion of preparation, and drank about four glasses to a piece instead of one, not to mention the something strong which went on the top of it. Whether the brass armour checked the natural flow of perspiration, and thus prevented the spirit from evaporating, we are not scientific enough to know; but, whatever the cause was, Mr. Twigger no sooner found himself outside the gate of Mudfog Hall, than he also found himself in a very considerable state of intoxication; and hence his extraordinary style of progressing. This was bad enough, but, as if fate and fortune had conspired against Nicholas Tulrumble, Mr. Twigger, not having been penitent for a good calendar month, took it into his head to be most especially and particularly sentimental, just when his repentance could have been most conveniently dispensed with. Immense tears were rolling down his cheeks, and he was vainly endeavouring to conceal his grief by applying to his eyes a blue cotton pocket-handkerchief with white spots, – an article not strictly in keeping with a suit of armour some three hundred years old, or thereabouts.

'Twigger, you villain!' said Nicholas Tulrumble, quite forgetting his dignity, 'go back.'

'Never,' said Ned. 'I'm a miserable wretch. I'll never leave you.'

The by-standers of course received this declaration with acclamations of 'That's right, Ned; don't!'

'I don't intend it,' said Ned, with all the obstinacy of a very tipsy man. 'I'm very unhappy. I'm the wretched father of an unfortunate family; but I am very faithful, sir. I'll never leave you.' Having reiterated this obliging promise, Ned proceeded in broken words to harangue the crowd upon the number of years he had lived in Mudfog, the excessive respectability of his character, and other topics of the like nature.

'Here! will anybody lead him away?' said Nicholas: 'if they'll call on me afterwards, I'll reward them well.'

Two or three men stepped forward, with the view of bearing Ned off, when the secretary interposed.

'Take care! take care!' said Mr. Jennings. 'I beg your pardon, sir; but they'd better not go too near him, because, if he falls over, he'll certainly crush somebody.'

At this hint the crowd retired on all sides to a very respectful distance, and left Ned, like the Duke of Devonshire, in a little circle of his own.

'But, Mr. Jennings,' said Nicholas Tulrumble, 'he'll be suffocated.'

'I'm very sorry for it, sir,' replied Mr. Jennings; 'but nobody can get that armour off, without his own assistance. I'm quite certain of it from the way he put it on.'

Here Ned wept dolefully, and shook his helmeted head, in a manner that might have touched a heart of stone; but the crowd had not hearts of stone, and they laughed heartily.

'Dear me, Mr. Jennings,' said Nicholas, turning pale at the possibility of Ned's being smothered in his antique costume – 'Dear me, Mr. Jennings, can nothing be done with him?'

'Nothing at all,' replied Ned, 'nothing at all. Gentlemen, I'm an unhappy wretch. I'm a body, gentlemen, in a brass coffin.' At this poetical idea of his own conjuring up, Ned cried so much that the people began to get sympathetic, and to ask what Nicholas Tulrumble meant by putting a man into such a machine as that; and one individual in a hairy waistcoat like the top of a trunk, who had previously expressed his opinion that if Ned hadn't been a poor man, Nicholas wouldn't have dared do it, hinted at the propriety of breaking the four-wheel chaise, or Nicholas's head, or both, which last compound proposition the crowd seemed to consider a very good notion.

It was not acted upon, however, for it had hardly been broached, when Ned Twigger's wife made her appearance abruptly in the little circle before noticed, and Ned no sooner caught a glimpse of her face and form, than from the mere force of habit he set off towards his home just as fast as his legs could carry him; and that was not very quick in the present instance either, for, however ready they might have been to carry *him*, they couldn't get on very well under the brass armour. So, Mrs. Twigger had plenty of time to denounce Nicholas Tulrumble to his face: to express her opinion that he was a decided monster; and to intimate that, if her ill-used husband sustained any personal damage from the brass armour, she would have the law of Nicholas Tulrumble for manslaughter. When she had said all this with due vehemence, she posted after Ned, who was dragging himself along as best he could, and deploring his unhappiness in most dismal tones.

What a wailing and screaming Ned's children raised when he got home at last! Mrs. Twigger tried to undo the armour, first in one place, and then in another, but she couldn't manage it; so she tumbled Ned into bed, helmet, armour, gauntlets, and all. Such a creaking as the bedstead made, under Ned's weight in his new suit! It didn't break down though; and there Ned lay, like the anonymous vessel in the Bay of Biscay, till next day, drinking barley-water, and looking miserable: and every time he groaned, his good lady said it served him right, which was all the consolation Ned Twigger got.

Nicholas Tulrumble and the gorgeous procession went on together to the town-hall, amid the hisses and groans of all the spectators, who had suddenly taken it into their heads to consider poor Ned a martyr. Nicholas was formally installed in his new office, in acknowledgment of which ceremony he delivered himself of a speech, composed by the secretary, which was very long, and no doubt very good, only the noise of the people outside prevented anybody from hearing it, but Nicholas Tulrumble himself. After which, the procession got back to Mudfog Hall any how it could; and Nicholas and the corporation sat down to dinner.

But the dinner was flat, and Nicholas was disappointed. They were such dull sleepy old fellows, that corporation. Nicholas made quite as long speeches as the Lord Mayor of London had done, nay, he said the very same things that the Lord Mayor of London had said, and the deuce a cheer the corporation gave him. There was only one man in the party who was thoroughly awake; and he was insolent, and called him Nick. Nick! What would be the consequence, thought Nicholas, of anybody presuming to call the Lord Mayor of London 'Nick!' He should like to know what the sword-bearer would say to that; or the recorder, or the toast-master, or any other of the great officers of the city. They'd nick him.

But these were not the worst of Nicholas Tulrumble's doings. If they had been, he might have remained a Mayor to this day, and have talked till he lost his voice. He contracted a relish for statistics, and got philosophical; and the statistics and the philosophy together, led him into an act which increased his unpopularity and hastened his downfall.

At the very end of the Mudfog High-street, and abutting on the river-side, stands the Jolly Boatmen, an old-fashioned low-roofed, bay-windowed house, with a bar, kitchen, and tap-room all in one, and a large fire-place with a kettle to correspond, round which the working men have congregated time out of mind on a winter's night, refreshed by draughts of good strong beer, and cheered by the sounds of a fiddle and tambourine: the Jolly Boatmen having been duly licensed by the Mayor and corporation, to scrape the fiddle and thumb the tambourine from time, whereof the memory of the oldest inhabitants goeth not to the contrary. Now Nicholas Tulrumble had been reading pamphlets on crime, and parliamentary reports, – or had made the secretary read them to him, which is the same thing in effect, – and he at once perceived that this fiddle and tambourine must have done more to demoralize Mudfog, than any other operating causes that ingenuity could imagine. So he read up for the subject, and determined to come out on the corporation with a burst, the very next time the licence was applied for.

The licensing day came, and the red-faced landlord of the Jolly Boatmen walked into the town-hall, looking as jolly as need be, having actually put on an extra fiddle for that night, to commemorate the anniversary of the Jolly Boatmen's music licence. It was applied for in due form, and was just about to be granted as a matter of course, when up rose Nicholas Tulrumble, and drowned the astonished corporation in a torrent of eloquence. He descanted in glowing terms upon the increasing depravity of his native town of Mudfog, and the excesses committed by its population. Then, he related how shocked he had been, to see barrels of beer sliding down into the cellar of the Jolly Boatmen week after week; and how he had sat at a window opposite the Jolly Boatmen for two days together, to count the people who went in for beer between the hours of twelve and one o'clock alone – which, by-the-bye, was the time at which the great majority of the Mudfog people dined. Then, he went on to state, how the number of people who came out with beer-jugs, averaged twenty-one in five minutes, which, being multiplied by twelve, gave two hundred and fifty-two people with beer-jugs in an hour, and multiplied again by fifteen (the number of hours during which the house was open daily) yielded three thousand seven hundred and eighty people with beer-jugs per day, or twenty-six thousand four hundred and sixty people with beer-jugs, per week. Then he proceeded to show that a tambourine and moral degradation were synonymous terms, and a fiddle and vicious propensities wholly inseparable. All these arguments he strengthened and demonstrated by frequent references to a large book with a blue cover, and sundry quotations from the Middlesex magistrates; and in the end, the corporation, who were posed with the figures, and sleepy with the speech, and sadly in want of dinner into the bargain, yielded the palm to Nicholas Tulrumble, and refused the music licence to the Jolly Boatmen.

But although Nicholas triumphed, his triumph was short. He carried on the war against beer-jugs and fiddles, forgetting the time when he was glad to drink out of the one, and to dance to the other, till the people hated, and his old friends shunned him. He grew tired of the lonely magnificence of Mudfog Hall, and his heart yearned towards the Lighterman's Arms. He wished he had never set up as a public man, and sighed for the good old times of the coal-shop, and the chimney corner.

At length old Nicholas, being thoroughly miserable, took heart of grace, paid the secretary a quarter's wages in advance, and packed him off to London by the next coach. Having taken this step, he put his hat on his head, and his pride in his pocket, and walked down to the old room at the Lighterman's Arms. There were only two of the old fellows there, and they looked coldly on Nicholas as he proffered his hand.

'Are you going to put down pipes, Mr. Tulrumble?' said one.

'Or trace the progress of crime to 'bacca?' growled the other.

'Neither,' replied Nicholas Tulrumble, shaking hands with them both, whether they would or not. 'I've come down to say that I'm very sorry for having made a fool of myself, and that I hope you'll give me up the old chair again.'

The old fellows opened their eyes, and three or four more old fellows opened the door, to whom Nicholas, with tears in his eyes, thrust out his hand too, and told the same story. They raised a shout of joy, that made the bells in the ancient church-tower vibrate again, and wheeling the old chair into the warm corner, thrust old Nicholas down into it, and ordered in the very largest-sized bowl of hot punch, with an unlimited number of pipes, directly.

The next day, the Jolly Boatmen got the licence, and the next night, old Nicholas and Ned Twigger's wife led off a dance to the music of the fiddle and tambourine, the tone of which seemed mightily improved by a little rest, for they never had played so merrily before. Ned Twigger was in the very height of his glory, and he danced hornpipes, and balanced chairs on his chin, and straws on his nose, till the whole company, including the corporation, were in raptures of admiration at the brilliancy of his acquirements.

Mr. Tulrumble, junior, couldn't make up his mind to be anything but magnificent, so he went up to London and drew bills on his father; and when he had overdrawn, and got into debt, he grew penitent, and came home again.

As to old Nicholas, he kept his word, and having had six weeks of public life, never tried it any more. He went to sleep in the town-hall at the very next meeting; and, in full proof of his sincerity, has requested us to write this faithful narrative. We wish it could have the effect of reminding the Tulrumbles of another sphere, that puffed-up conceit is not dignity, and that snarling at the little pleasures they were once glad to enjoy, because they would rather forget the times when they were of lower station, renders them objects of contempt and ridicule.

This is the first time we have published any of our gleanings from this particular source. Perhaps, at some future period, we may venture to open the chronicles of Mudfog.

FULL REPORT OF THE FIRST MEETING
OF THE MUDFOG ASSOCIATION
FOR THE ADVANCEMENT OF EVERYTHING

We have made the most unparalleled and extraordinary exertions to place before our readers a complete and accurate account of the proceedings at the late grand meeting of the Mudfog Association, holden in the town of Mudfog; it affords us great happiness to lay the result before them, in the shape of various communications received from our able, talented, and graphic correspondent, expressly sent down for the purpose, who has immortalized us, himself, Mudfog, and the association, all at one and the same time. We have been, indeed, for some days unable to determine who will transmit the greatest name to posterity; ourselves, who sent our correspondent down; our correspondent, who wrote an account of the matter; or the association, who gave our correspondent something to write about. We rather incline to the opinion that we are the greatest man of the party, inasmuch as the notion of an exclusive and authentic report originated with us; this may be prejudice: it may arise from a prepossession on our part in our own favour. Be it so. We have no doubt that every gentleman concerned in this mighty assemblage is troubled with the same complaint in a greater or less degree; and it is a consolation to us to know that we have at least this feeling in common with the great scientific stars, the brilliant and extraordinary luminaries, whose speculations we record.

We give our correspondent's letters in the order in which they reached us. Any attempt at amalgamating them into one beautiful whole, would only destroy that glowing tone, that dash of wildness, and rich vein of picturesque interest, which pervade them throughout.

'*Mudfog, Monday night, seven o'clock.*

'We are in a state of great excitement here. Nothing is spoken of, but the approaching meeting of the association. The inn-doors are thronged with waiters anxiously looking for the expected arrivals; and the numerous bills which are wafered up in the windows of private houses, intimating that there are beds to let within, give the streets a very animated and cheerful appearance, the wafers being of a great variety of colours, and the monotony of printed inscriptions being relieved by every possible size and style of hand-writing. It is confidently rumoured that Professors Snore, Doze, and Wheezy have engaged three beds and a sitting-room at the Pig and Tinder-box. I give you the rumour as it has reached me; but I cannot, as yet, vouch for its accuracy. The moment I have been enabled to obtain any certain information upon this interesting point, you may depend upon receiving it.'

'*Half past seven.*

'I have just returned from a personal interview with the landlord of the Pig and Tinder-box. He speaks confidently of the probability of Professors Snore, Doze, and Wheezy taking up their residence at his house during the sitting of the association, but denies that the beds have been yet engaged; in which representation he is confirmed by the chambermaid – a girl of artless manners, and interesting appearance. The boots denies that it is at all likely that Professors Snore, Doze, and Wheezy will put up here; but I have reason to believe that this man has been suborned by the proprietor of the Original Pig, which is the opposition hotel. Amidst such conflicting testimony it is difficult to arrive at the real truth; but you may depend upon receiving authentic information upon this point the moment the fact is ascertained. The excitement still continues. A boy fell through the window of the pastrycook's shop at the corner of the High-street about half an hour ago, which has occasioned much confusion. The general impression is, that it was an accident. Pray heaven it may prove so!'

'Tuesday, noon.

'At an early hour this morning the bells of all the churches struck seven o'clock; the effect of which, in the present lively state of the town, was extremely singular. While I was at breakfast, a yellow gig, drawn by a dark grey horse, with a patch of white over his right eyelid, proceeded at a rapid pace in the direction of the Original Pig stables; it is currently reported that this gentleman has arrived here for the purpose of attending the association, and, from what I have heard, I consider it extremely probable, although nothing decisive is yet known regarding him. You may conceive the anxiety with which we are all looking forward to the arrival of the four o'clock coach this afternoon.

'Notwithstanding the excited state of the populace, no outrage has yet been committed, owing to the admirable discipline and discretion of the police, who are nowhere to be seen. A barrel-organ is playing opposite my window, and groups of people, offering fish and vegetables for sale, parade the streets. With these exceptions everything is quiet, and I trust will continue so.'

'Five o'clock.

'It is now ascertained, beyond all doubt, that Professors Snore, Doze, and Wheezy will *not* repair to the Pig and Tinder-box, but have actually engaged apartments at the Original Pig. This intelligence is *exclusive*; and I leave you and your readers to draw their own inferences from it. Why Professor Wheezy, of all people in the world, should repair to the Original Pig in preference to the Pig and Tinder-box, it is not easy to conceive. The professor is a man who should be above all such petty feelings. Some people here openly impute treachery, and a distinct breach of faith to Professors Snore and Doze; while others, again, are disposed to acquit them of any culpability in the transaction, and to insinuate that the blame rests solely with Professor Wheezy. I own that I incline to the latter opinion; and although it gives me great pain to speak in terms of censure or disapprobation of a man of such transcendent genius and acquirements, still I am bound to say that, if my suspicions be well founded, and if all the reports which have reached my ears be true, I really do not well know what to make of the matter.

'Mr. Slug, so celebrated for his statistical researches, arrived this afternoon by the four o'clock stage. His complexion is a dark purple, and he has a habit of sighing constantly. He looked extremely well, and appeared in high health and spirits. Mr. Woodensconse also came down in the same conveyance. The distinguished gentleman was fast asleep on his arrival, and I am informed by the guard that he had been so the whole way. He was, no doubt, preparing for his approaching fatigues; but what gigantic visions must those be that flit through the brain of such a man when his body is in a state of torpidity!

'The influx of visitors increases every moment. I am told (I know not how truly) that two post-chaises have arrived at the Original Pig within the last half-hour, and I myself observed a wheelbarrow, containing three carpet bags and a bundle, entering the yard of the Pig and Tinder-box no longer ago than five minutes since. The people are still quietly pursuing their ordinary occupations; but there is a wildness in their eyes, and an unwonted rigidity in the muscles of their countenances, which shows to the observant spectator that their expectations are strained to the very utmost pitch. I fear, unless some very extraordinary arrivals take place tonight, that consequences may arise from this popular ferment, which every man of sense and feeling would deplore.'

'*Twenty minutes past six.*

'I have just heard that the boy who fell through the pastrycook's window last night has died of the fright. He was suddenly called upon to pay three and sixpence for the damage done, and his constitution, it seems, was not strong enough to bear up against the shock. The inquest, it is said, will be held tomorrow.'

'*Three-quarters past seven.*

'Professors Muff and Nogo have just driven up to the hotel door; they at once ordered dinner with great condescension. We are all very much delighted with the urbanity of their manners, and the ease with which they adapt themselves to the forms and ceremonies of ordinary life. Immediately on their arrival they sent for the head waiter, and privately requested him to purchase a live dog, – as cheap a one as he could meet with, – and to send him up after dinner, with a pie-board, a knife and fork, and a clean plate. It is conjectured that some experiments will be tried upon the dog tonight; if any particulars should transpire, I will forward them by express.'

'*Half-past eight.*

'The animal has been procured. He is a pug-dog, of rather intelligent appearance, in good condition, and with very short legs. He has been tied to a curtain-peg in a dark room, and is howling dreadfully.'

'*Ten minutes to nine.*

'The dog has just been rung for. With an instinct which would appear almost the result of reason, the sagacious animal seized the waiter by the calf of the leg when he approached to take him, and made a desperate, though ineffectual resistance. I have not been able to procure admission to the apartment occupied by the scientific gentlemen; but, judging from the sounds which reached my ears when I stood upon the landing-place outside the door, just now, I should be disposed to say that the dog had retreated growling beneath some article of furniture, and was keeping the professors at bay. This conjecture is confirmed by the testimony of the ostler, who, after peeping through the keyhole, assures me that he distinctly saw Professor Nogo on his knees, holding forth a small bottle of prussic acid, to which the animal, who was crouched beneath an arm-chair, obstinately declined to smell. You cannot imagine the feverish state of irritation we are in, lest the interests of science should be sacrificed to the prejudices of a brute creature, who is not endowed with sufficient sense to foresee the incalculable benefits which the whole human race may derive from so very slight a concession on his part.'

'Nine o'clock.

'The dog's tail and ears have been sent down stairs to be washed; from which circumstance we infer that the animal is no more. His forelegs have been delivered to the boots to be brushes, which strengthens the supposition.'

'Half after ten.

'My feelings are so overpowered by what has taken place in the course of the last hour and a half, that I have scarcely strength to detail the rapid succession of events which have quite bewildered all those who are cognizant of their occurrence. It appears that the pug-dog mentioned in my last was surreptitiously obtained, – stolen, in fact, – by some person attached to the stable department, from an unmarried lady resident in this town. Frantic on discovering the loss of her favourite, the lady rushed distractedly into the street, calling in the most heart-rending and pathetic manner upon the passengers to restore her, her Augustus, – for so the deceased was named, in affectionate remembrance of a former lover of his mistress, to whom he bore a striking personal resemblance, which renders the circumstances additionally affecting. I am not yet in a condition to inform you what circumstance induced the bereaved lady to direct her steps to the hotel which had witnessed the last struggles of her *protégé*. I can only state that she arrived there, at the very instant when his detached members were passing through the passage on a small tray. Her shrieks still reverberate in my ears! I grieve to say that the expressive features of Professor Muff were much scratched and lacerated by the injured lady; and that Professor Nogo, besides sustaining several severe bites, has lost some handfuls of hair from the same cause. It must be some consolation to these gentlemen to know that their ardent attachment to scientific pursuits has alone occasioned these unpleasant consequences; for which the sympathy of a grateful country will sufficiently reward them. The unfortunate lady remains at the Pig and Tinder-box, and up to this time is reported in a very precarious state.

'I need scarcely tell you that this unlooked-for catastrophe has cast a damp and gloom upon us in the midst of our exhilaration; natural in any case, but greatly enhanced in this, by the amiable qualities of the deceased animal, who appears to have been much and deservedly respected by the whole of his acquaintance.'

'*Twelve o'clock.*

'I take the last opportunity before sealing my parcel to inform you that the boy who fell through the pastrycook's window is not dead, as was universally believed, but alive and well. The report appears to have had its origin in his mysterious disappearance. He was found half an hour since on the premises of a sweet-stuff maker, where a raffle had been announced for a second-hand seal-skin cap and a tambourine;

and where – a sufficient number of members not having been obtained at first – he had patiently waited until the list was completed. This fortunate discovery has in some degree restored our gaiety and cheerfulness. It is proposed to get up a subscription for him without delay.

'Everybody is nervously anxious to see what tomorrow will bring forth. If any one should arrive in the course of the night, I have left strict directions to be called immediately. I should have sat up, indeed, but the agitating events of this day have been too much for me.

'No news yet of either of the Professors Snore, Doze, or Wheezy. It is very strange!'

'*Wednesday afternoon.*

'All is now over; and, upon one point at least, I am at length enabled to set the minds of your readers at rest. The three professors arrived at ten minutes after two o'clock, and, instead of taking up their quarters at the Original Pig, as it was universally understood in the course of yesterday that they would assuredly have done, drove straight to the Pig and Tinder-box, where they threw off the mask at once, and openly announced their intention of remaining. Professor Wheezy *may* reconcile this very extraordinary conduct with *his* notions of fair and equitable dealing, but I would recommend Professor Wheezy to be cautious how he presumes too far upon his well-earned reputation. How such a man as Professor Snore, or, which is still more extraordinary, such an individual as Professor Doze, can quietly allow himself to be mixed up with such proceedings as these, you will naturally inquire. Upon this head, rumour is silent; I have my speculations, but forbear to give utterance to them just now.'

'*Four o'clock.*

'The town is filling fast; eighteenpence has been offered for a bed and refused. Several gentlemen were under the necessity last night of sleeping in the brick fields, and on the steps of doors, for which they were taken before the magistrates in a body this morning, and committed to prison as vagrants for various terms. One of these persons I understand to be a highly-respectable tinker, of great practical skill, who had forwarded a paper to the President of Section D. Mechanical Science, on the construction of pipkins with copper bottoms and safety-valves, of which report speaks highly. The incarceration of this gentleman is greatly to be regretted, as his absence will preclude any discussion on the subject.

'The bills are being taken down in all directions, and lodgings are being secured on almost any terms. I have heard of fifteen shillings a week for two rooms, exclusive of coals and attendance, but I can scarcely believe it. The excitement is dreadful. I was informed this morning that the civil authorities, apprehensive of some outbreak of popular feeling, had commanded a recruiting sergeant and two corporals to be under arms; and that, with the view of not irritating the people unnecessarily by their presence, they had been requested to take up their position before daybreak in a turnpike, distant about a quarter of a mile from the town. The vigour and promptness of these measures cannot be too highly extolled.

'Intelligence has just been brought me, that an elderly female, in a state of inebriety, has declared in the open street her intention to "do" for Mr. Slug. Some statistical returns compiled by that gentleman, relative to the consumption of raw spirituous liquors in this place, are supposed to be the cause of the wretch's animosity. It is added that this declaration was loudly cheered by a crowd of persons who had assembled on the spot; and that one man had the boldness to designate Mr. Slug aloud by the opprobrious epithet of 'Stick-in-the-mud!' It is earnestly to be hoped that now, when the moment has arrived for their interference, the magistrates will not shrink from the exercise of that power which is vested in them by the constitution of our common country.'

'*Half-past ten.*

'The disturbance, I am happy to inform you, has been completely quelled, and the ringleader taken into custody. She had a pail of cold water thrown over her, previous to being locked up, and expresses great contrition and uneasiness. We are all in a fever of anticipation about tomorrow; but, now that we are within a few hours of the meeting of the association, and at last enjoy the proud consciousness of having its illustrious members amongst us, I trust and hope everything may go off peaceably. I shall send you a full report of tomorrow's proceedings by the night coach.'

'*Eleven o'clock.*

'I open my letter to say that nothing whatever has occurred since I folded it up.'

'*Thursday.*

'The sun rose this morning at the usual hour. I did not observe anything particular in the aspect of the glorious planet, except that he appeared to me (it might have been a delusion of my heightened fancy) to shine with more than common brilliancy, and to shed a refulgent lustre upon the town, such as I had never observed before. This is the more extraordinary, as the sky was perfectly cloudless, and the atmosphere peculiarly fine. At half-past nine o'clock the general committee assembled, with the last year's president in the chair. The report of the council was read; and one passage, which stated that the council had corresponded with no less than three thousand five hundred and seventy-one persons, (all of whom paid their own postage,) on no fewer than seven thousand two hundred and forty-three topics, was received with a degree of enthusiasm which no efforts could suppress.

The various committees and sections having been appointed, and the more formal business transacted, the great proceedings of the meeting commenced at eleven o'clock precisely. I had the happiness of occupying a most eligible position at that time, in

'SECTION A. – ZOOLOGY AND BOTANY.

GREAT ROOM, PIG AND TINDER-BOX.

President – Professor Snore. *Vice-Presidents* – Professors Doze and Wheezy.

'The scene at this moment was particularly striking. The sun streamed through the windows of the apartments, and tinted the whole scene with its brilliant rays, bringing out in strong relief the noble visages of the professors and scientific gentlemen, who, some with bald heads, some with red heads, some with brown heads, some with grey heads, some with black heads, some with block heads, presented a *coup d'œil* which no eye-witness will readily forget. In front of these gentlemen were papers and inkstands; and round the room, on elevated benches extending as far as the forms could reach, were assembled a brilliant concourse of those lovely and elegant women for which Mudfog is justly acknowledged to be without a rival in the whole world. The contrast between their fair faces and the dark coats and trousers of the scientific gentlemen I shall never cease to remember while Memory holds her seat.

'Time having been allowed for a slight confusion, occasioned by the falling down of the greater part of the platforms, to subside, the president called on one of the secretaries to read a communication entitled, "Some remarks on the industrious fleas, with considerations on the importance of establishing infant-schools among that numerous class of society; of directing their industry to useful and practical ends; and of applying the surplus fruits thereof, towards providing for them a comfortable and respectable maintenance in their old age."

'The author stated, that, having long turned his attention to the moral and social condition of these interesting animals, he had been induced to visit an exhibition in Regent-street, London, commonly known by the designation of "The Industrious Fleas." He had there seen many fleas, occupied certainly in various pursuits and avocations, but occupied, he was bound to add, in a manner which no man of well-regulated mind could fail to regard with sorrow and regret. One flea, reduced to the level of a beast of burden, was drawing about a miniature gig, containing a particularly small effigy of His Grace the Duke of Wellington; while another was staggering beneath the weight of a golden model of his great adversary Napoleon Bonaparte. Some, brought up as mountebanks and ballet-dancers, were performing a figure-dance (he regretted to observe, that, of the fleas so employed, several were females); others were in training, in a small cardboard box, for pedestrians, – mere sporting characters – and two were actually engaged in the cold-blooded and barbarous occupation of duelling; a pursuit from which humanity recoiled with horror and disgust. He suggested that measures should be immediately taken to employ the labour of these fleas as part and parcel of the productive power of the country, which might easily be done by the establishment among them of infant schools and houses of industry, in which a system of virtuous education, based upon sound principles, should be observed, and moral precepts strictly inculcated. He proposed that every flea who presumed to exhibit, for hire, music, or dancing, or any species of theatrical entertainment, without a licence, should be considered a vagabond, and treated accordingly; in which respect he only placed him upon a level with the rest of mankind. He would further suggest that their labour should be placed under the control and regulation of the state, who should set apart from the profits, a fund for the support of superannuated or disabled fleas, their widows and orphans. With this view, he proposed that liberal premiums should be offered for the three best designs for a general almshouse; from which – as insect architecture was well known to be in a very advanced and perfect state – we might possibly derive many valuable hints for the improvement of our metropolitan universities, national galleries, and other public edifices.

'The President wished to be informed how the ingenious gentleman proposed to open a communication with fleas generally, in the first instance, so that they might be thoroughly imbued with a sense of the advantages they must necessarily derive from changing their mode of life, and applying themselves to honest labour. This appeared to him, the only difficulty.

'The Author submitted that this difficulty was easily overcome, or rather that there was no difficulty at all in the case. Obviously the course to be pursued, if Her Majesty's government could be prevailed upon to take up the plan, would be, to secure at a remunerative salary the individual to whom he had alluded as presiding over the exhibition in Regent-street at the period of his visit. That gentleman would at once be able to put himself in communication with the mass of the fleas, and to instruct them in pursuance of some general plan of education, to be sanctioned by Parliament, until such time as the more intelligent among them were advanced enough to officiate as teachers to the rest.

'The President and several members of the section highly complimented the author of the paper last read, on his most ingenious and important treatise. It was determined that the subject should be recommended to the immediate consideration of the council.

'Mr. Wigsby produced a cauliflower somewhat larger than a chaise-umbrella, which had been raised by no other artificial means than the simple application of highly carbonated soda-water as manure. He explained that by scooping out the head, which would afford a new and delicious species of nourishment for the poor, a parachute, in principle something similar to that constructed by M. Garnerin, was at once obtained; the stalk of course being kept downwards. He added that he was perfectly willing to make a descent from a height of not less than three miles and a quarter; and had in fact already proposed the same to the proprietors of Vauxhall Gardens, who in the handsomest manner at once consented to his wishes, and appointed an early day next summer for the undertaking; merely stipulating that the rim of the cauliflower should be previously broken in three or four places to ensure the safety of the descent.

'The President congratulated the public on the *grand gala* in store for them, and warmly eulogised the proprietors of the establishment alluded to, for their love of science, and regard for the safety of human life, both of which did them the highest honour.

'A Member wished to know how many thousand additional lamps the royal property would be illuminated with, on the night after the descent.

'Mr. Wigsby replied that the point was not yet finally decided; but he believed it was proposed, over and above the ordinary illuminations, to exhibit in various devices eight millions and a-half of additional lamps.

'The Member expressed himself much gratified with this announcement.

'Mr. Blunderum delighted the section with a most interesting and valuable paper "on the last moments of the learned pig," which produced a very strong impression on the assembly, the account being compiled from the personal recollections of his favourite attendant. The account stated in the most emphatic terms that the animal's name was not Toby, but Solomon; and distinctly proved that he could have no near relatives in the profession, as many designing persons had falsely stated, inasmuch as his father, mother, brothers and sisters, had all fallen victims to the butcher at different times. An uncle of his indeed, had with very great labour been traced to a sty in Somers Town; but as he was in a very infirm state at the time, being afflicted with measles, and shortly afterwards disappeared, there appeared too much reason to conjecture that he had been converted into sausages. The disorder of the learned pig was originally a severe cold, which, being aggravated by excessive trough indulgence, finally settled upon the lungs, and terminated in a general decay of the constitution. A melancholy instance of a presentiment entertained by the animal of his approaching dissolution, was recorded. After gratifying a numerous and fashionable company with his performances, in which no falling off whatever was visible, he fixed his eyes on the biographer, and, turning to the watch which lay on the floor, and on which he was accustomed to point out the hour, deliberately passed his snout twice round the dial. In precisely four-and-twenty hours from that time he had ceased to exist!

'Professor Wheezy inquired whether, previous to his demise, the animal had expressed, by signs or otherwise, any wishes regarding the disposal of his little property.

'Mr. Blunderum replied, that, when the biographer took up the pack of cards at the conclusion of the performance, the animal grunted several times in a significant manner, nodding his head as he was accustomed to do, when gratified. From these gestures it was understood that he wished the attendant to keep the cards, which he had ever since done. He had not expressed any wish relative to his watch, which had accordingly been pawned by the same individual.

'The President wished to know whether any Member of the section had ever seen or conversed with the pig-faced lady, who was reported to have worn a black velvet mask, and to have taken her meals from a golden trough.

'After some hesitation a Member replied that the pig-faced lady was his mother-in-law, and that he trusted the President would not violate the sanctity of private life.

'The President begged pardon. He had considered the pig-faced lady a public character. Would the honourable member object to state, with a view to the advancement of science, whether she was in any way connected with the learned pig?

'The Member replied in the same low tone, that, as the question appeared to involve a suspicion that the learned pig might be his half-brother, he must decline answering it.

'SECTION B. – ANATOMY AND MEDICINE.

COACH-HOUSE, PIG AND TINDER-BOX.

President – Dr. Toorell. *Vice-Presidents* – Professors Muff and Nogo.

'Dr. Kutankumagen (of Moscow) read to the section a report of a case which had occurred within his own practice, strikingly illustrative of the power of medicine, as exemplified in his successful treatment of a virulent disorder. He had been called in to visit the patient on the 1st of April 1837. He was then labouring under symptoms peculiarly alarming to any medical man. His frame was stout and muscular, his step firm and elastic, his cheeks plump and red, his voice loud, his appetite good, his pulse full and round. He was in the constant habit of eating three meals *per diem*, and of drinking at least one bottle of wine, and one glass of spirituous liquors diluted with water, in the course of the four-and-twenty hours. He laughed constantly, and in so hearty a manner that it was terrible to hear him. By dint of powerful medicine, low diet, and bleeding, the symptoms in the course of three days perceptibly decreased. A rigid perseverance in the same course of treatment for only one week, accompanied with small doses of water-gruel, weak broth, and barley-water, led to their entire disappearance. In the course of a month he was sufficiently recovered to be carried down stairs by two nurses, and to enjoy an airing in a close carriage, supported by soft pillows. At the present moment he was restored so far as to walk about, with the slight assistance of a crutch and a boy. It would perhaps be gratifying to the section to learn that he ate little, drank little, slept little, and was never heard to laugh by any accident whatever.

'Dr. W.R. Fee, in complimenting the honourable member upon the triumphant cure he had effected, begged to ask whether the patient still bled freely?

'Dr. Kutankumagen replied in the affirmative.

'Dr. W.R. Fee. – And you found that he bled freely during the whole course of the disorder?

'Dr. Kutankumagen. – Oh dear, yes; most freely.

'Dr. Neeshawts supposed, that if the patient had not submitted to be bled with great readiness and perseverance, so extraordinary a cure could never, in fact, have been accomplished. Dr. Kutankumagen rejoined, certainly not.

'Mr. Knight Bell (M.R.C.S.) exhibited a wax preparation of the interior of a gentleman who in early life had inadvertently swallowed a door-key. It was a curious fact that a medical student of dissipated habits, being present at the *post mortem* examination, found means to escape unobserved from the room, with that portion of the coats of the stomach upon which an exact model of the instrument was distinctly impressed, with which he hastened to a locksmith of doubtful character, who made a new key from the pattern so shown to him. With this key the medical student entered the house of the deceased gentleman, and committed a burglary to a large amount, for which he was subsequently tried and executed.

'The President wished to know what became of the original key after the lapse of years. Mr. Knight Bell replied that the gentleman was always much accustomed to punch, and it was supposed the acid had gradually devoured it.

'Dr. Neeshawts and several of the members were of opinion that the key must have lain very cold and heavy upon the gentleman's stomach.

'Mr. Knight Bell believed it did at first. It was worthy of remark, perhaps, that for some years the gentleman was troubled with a night-mare, under the influence of which he always imagined himself a wine-cellar door.

'Professor Muff related a very extraordinary and convincing proof of the wonderful efficacy of the system of infinitesimal doses, which the section were doubtless aware was based upon the theory that the very minutest amount of any given drug, properly dispersed through the human frame, would be productive of precisely the same result as a very large dose administered in the usual manner. Thus, the fortieth part of a grain of calomel was supposed to be equal to a five-grain calomel pill, and so on in proportion throughout the whole range of medicine. He had tried the experiment in a curious manner upon a publican who had been brought into the hospital with a broken head, and was cured upon the infinitesimal system in the incredibly short space of three months. This man was a hard drinker. He (Professor Muff) had dispersed three drops of rum through a bucket of water, and requested the man to drink the whole. What was the result? Before he had drunk a quart, he was in a state of beastly intoxication; and five other men were made dead drunk with the remainder.

'The President wished to know whether an infinitesimal dose of soda-water would have recovered them? Professor Muff replied that the twenty-fifth part of a teaspoonful, properly administered to each patient, would have sobered him immediately. The President remarked that this was a most important discovery, and he hoped the Lord Mayor and Court of Aldermen would patronize it immediately.

'A Member begged to be informed whether it should be possible to administer – say, the twentieth part of a grain of bread and cheese to all grown-up paupers, and the fortieth part to children, with the same satisfying effect as their present allowance.

'Professor Muff was willing to stake his professional reputation on the perfect adequacy of such a quantity of food to the support of human life – in workhouses; the addition of the fifteenth part of a grain of pudding twice a week would render it a high diet.

'Professor Nogo called the attention of the section to a very extraordinary case of animal magnetism. A private watchman, being merely looked at by the operator from the opposite side of a wide street, was at once observed to be in a very drowsy and languid state. He was followed to his box, and being once slightly rubbed on the palms of the hands, fell into a sound sleep, in which he continued without intermission for ten hours.

'SECTION C. – STATISTICS.

HAY-LOFT, ORIGINAL PIG.

President – Mr. Woodensconce. *Vice-Presidents* – Mr. Ledbrain and Mr. Timbered.

'Mr. Slug stated to the section the result of some calculations he had made with great difficulty and labour, regarding the state of infant education among the middle classes of London. He found that, within a circle of three miles from the Elephant and Castle, the following were the names and numbers of children's books principally in circulation:–

'Jack the Giant-killer	7,943
Ditto and Bean-stalk	8,621
Ditto and Eleven Brothers	2,845
Ditto and Jill	1,998
Total	21,407

'He found that the proportion of Robinson Crusoes to Philip Quarlls was as four and a half to one; and that the preponderance of Valentine and Orsons over Goody Two Shoeses was as three and an eighth of the former to half a one of the latter; a comparison of Seven Champions with Simple Simons gave the same result. The ignorance that prevailed, was lamentable. One child, on being asked whether he would rather be Saint George of England or a respectable tallow-chandler, instantly replied, "Taint George of Ingling." Another, a little boy of eight years old, was found to be firmly impressed with a belief in the existence of dragons, and openly stated that it was his intention when he grew up, to rush forth sword in hand for the deliverance of captive princesses, and the promiscuous slaughter of giants. Not one child among the number interrogated had ever heard of Mungo Park, – some inquiring whether he was at all connected with the black man that swept the crossing; and others whether he was in any way related to the Regents Park. They had not the slightest conception of the commonest principles of mathematics, and considered Sinbad the Sailor the most enterprising voyager that the world had ever produced.

'A Member strongly deprecating the use of all the other books mentioned, suggested that Jack and Jill might perhaps be exempted from the general censure, inasmuch as the hero and heroine, in the very outset of the tale, were depicted as going *up* a hill to fetch a pail of water, which was a laborious and useful occupation, – supposing the family linen was being washed, for instance.

'Mr. Slug feared that the moral effect of this passage was more than counterbalanced by another in a subsequent part of the poem, in which very gross allusion was made to the mode in which the heroine was personally chastised by her mother

'"For laughing at Jack's disaster;"

besides, the whole work had this one great fault, *it was not true.*

'The President complimented the honourable member on the excellent distinction he had drawn. Several other Members, too, dwelt upon the immense and urgent necessity of storing the minds of children with nothing but facts and figures; which process the President very forcibly remarked, had made them (the section) the men they were.

'Mr. Slug then stated some curious calculations respecting the dogs'-meat barrows of London. He found that the total number of small carts and barrows engaged in dispensing provision to the cats and dogs of the metropolis was one thousand seven hundred and forty-three. The average number of skewers delivered daily with the provender, by each dogs'-meat cart or barrow, was thirty-six. Now, multiplying the number of skewers so delivered by the number of barrows, a total of sixty-two thousand seven hundred and forty-eight skewers daily would be obtained. Allowing that, of these sixty-two thousand seven hundred and forty-eight skewers, the odd two thousand seven hundred and forty-eight were accidentally devoured with the meat, by the most voracious of the animals supplied, it followed that sixty thousand skewers per day, or the enormous number of twenty-one millions nine hundred thousand skewers annually, were wasted in the kennels and dustholes of London; which, if collected and warehoused, would in ten years' time afford a mass of timber more than sufficient for the construction of a first-rate vessel of war for the use of Her Majesty's navy, to be called "The Royal Skewer," and to become under that name the terror of all the enemies of this island.

'Mr. X. Ledbrain read a very ingenious communication, from which it appeared that the total number of legs belonging to the manufacturing populations of one great town in Yorkshire was, in round numbers, forty thousand, while the total number of chair and stool legs in their houses was only thirty thousand, which, upon the very favourable average of three legs to a seat, yielded only ten thousand seats in all. From this calculation it would appear, – not taking wooden or cork legs into the account, but allowing two legs to every person, – that ten thousand individuals (one-half of the whole population) were either destitute of any rest for their legs at all, or passed the whole of their leisure time in sitting upon boxes.

'SECTION D. – MECHANICAL SCIENCE.

COACH-HOUSE, ORIGINAL PIG.

President – Mr. Carter. *Vice-Presidents* – Mr. Truck and Mr. Waghorn.

'Professor Queerspeck exhibited an elegant model of a portable railway, neatly mounted in a green case, for the waistcoat pocket. By attaching this beautiful instrument to his boots, any Bank or public-office clerk could transport himself from his place of residence to his place of business, at the easy rate of sixty-five miles an hour, which, to gentlemen of sedentary pursuits, would be an incalculable advantage.

'The President was desirous of knowing whether it was necessary to have a level surface on which the gentleman was to run.

'Professor Queerspeck explained that City gentlemen would run in trains, being handcuffed together to prevent confusion or unpleasantness. For instance, trains would start every morning at eight, nine, and ten o'clock, from Camden Town, Islington, Camberwell, Hackney, and various other places in which City gentlemen are accustomed to reside. It would be necessary to have a level, but he had provided for this difficulty by proposing that the best line that the circumstances would admit of, should be taken through the sewers which undermine the streets of the metropolis, and which, well lighted by jets from the gas pipes which run immediately above them, would form a pleasant and commodious arcade, especially in winter-time, when the inconvenient custom of carrying umbrellas, now so general, could be wholly dispensed with. In reply to another question, Professor Queerspeck stated that no substitute for the purposes to which these arcades were at present devoted had yet occurred to him, but that he hoped no fanciful objection on this head would be allowed to interfere with so great an undertaking.

'Mr. Jobba produced a forcing-machine on a novel plan, for bringing joint-stock railway shares prematurely to a premium. The instrument was in the form of an elegant gilt weather-glass, of most dazzling appearance, and was worked behind, by strings, after the manner of a pantomime trick, the strings being always pulled by the directors of the company to which the machine belonged. The quicksilver was so ingeniously placed, that when the acting directors held shares in their pockets, figures denoting very small expenses and very large returns appeared upon the glass; but the moment the directors parted with these pieces of paper, the estimate of needful expenditure suddenly increased itself to an immense extent, while the statements of certain profits became reduced in the same proportion. Mr. Jobba stated that the machine had been in constant requisition for some months past, and he had never once known it to fail.

'A Member expressed his opinion that it was extremely neat and pretty. He wished to know whether it was not liable to accidental derangement? Mr. Jobba said that the whole machine was undoubtedly liable to be blown up, but that was the only objection to it.

'Professor Nogo arrived from the anatomical section to exhibit a model of a safety fire-escape, which could be fixed at any time, in less than half an hour, and by means of which, the youngest or most infirm persons (successfully resisting the progress of the flames until it was quite ready) could be preserved if they merely balanced themselves for a few minutes on the sill of their bed-room window, and got into the escape without falling into the street. The Professor stated that the number of boys who had been rescued in the daytime by this machine from houses which were not on fire, was almost incredible. Not a conflagration had occurred in the whole of London for many months past to which the escape had not been carried on the very next day, and put in action before a concourse of persons.

'The President inquired whether there was not some difficulty in ascertaining which was the top of the machine, and which the bottom, in cases of pressing emergency.

'Professor Nogo explained that of course it could not be expected to act quite as well when there was a fire, as when there was not a fire; but in the former case he thought it would be of equal service whether the top were up or down.'

With the last section our correspondent concludes his most able and faithful Report, which will never cease to reflect credit upon him for his scientific attainments, and upon us for our enterprising spirit. It is needless to take a review of the subjects which have been discussed; of the mode in which they have been examined; of the great truths which they have elicited. They are now before the world, and we leave them to read, to consider, and to profit.

The place of meeting for next year has undergone discussion, and has at length been decided, regard being had to, and evidence being taken upon, the goodness of its wines, the supply of its markets, the hospitality of its inhabitants, and the quality of its hotels. We hope at this next meeting our correspondent may again be present, and that we may be once more the means of placing his communications before the world. Until that period we have been prevailed upon to allow this number of our Miscellany to be retailed to the public, or wholesaled to the trade, without any advance upon our usual price.

We have only to add, that the committees are now broken up, and that Mudfog is once again restored to its accustomed tranquillity, – that Professors and Members have had balls, and *soirées*, and suppers, and great mutual complimentations, and have at length dispersed to their several homes, – whither all good wishes and joys attend them, until next year!

Signed   Boz.

FULL
REPORT OF THE SECOND MEETING
OF THE MUDFOG ASSOCIATION
FOR THE ADVANCEMENT OF EVERYTHING

In October last, we did ourselves the immortal credit of recording, at an enormous expense, and by dint of exertions unparalleled in the history of periodical publication, the proceedings of the Mudfog Association for the Advancement of Everything, which in that month held its first great half-yearly meeting, to the wonder and delight of the whole empire. We announced at the conclusion of that extraordinary and most remarkable Report, that when the Second Meeting of the Society should take place, we should be found again at our post, renewing our gigantic and spirited endeavours, and once more making the world ring with the accuracy, authenticity, immeasurable superiority, and intense remarkability of our account of its proceedings. In redemption of this pledge, we caused to be despatched per steam to Oldcastle (at which place this second meeting of the Society was held on the 20th instant), the same superhumanly-endowed gentleman who furnished the former report, and who, – gifted by nature with transcendent abilities, and furnished by us with a body of assistants scarcely inferior to himself, – has forwarded a series of letters, which, for faithfulness of description, power of language, fervour of thought, happiness of expression, and importance of subject-matter, have no equal in the epistolary literature of any age or country. We give this gentleman's correspondence entire, and in the order in which it reached our office.

'*Saloon of Steamer, Thursday night, half-past eight.*

'When I left new Burlington Street this evening in the hackney cabriolet, number four thousand two hundred and eighty-five, I experienced sensations as novel as they were oppressive. A sense of the importance of the task I had undertaken, a consciousness that I was leaving London, and, stranger still, going somewhere else, a feeling of loneliness and a sensation of jolting, quite bewildered my thoughts, and for a time rendered me even insensible to the presence of my carpet-bag and hat-box. I shall ever feel grateful to the driver of a Blackwall omnibus who, by thrusting the pole of his vehicle through the small door of the cabriolet, awakened me from a tumult of imaginings that are wholly indescribable. But of such materials is our imperfect nature composed!

'I am happy to say that I am the first passenger on board, and shall thus be enabled to give you an account of all that happens in the order of its occurrence. The chimney is smoking a good deal, and so are the crew; and the captain, I am informed, is very drunk in a little house upon deck, something like a black turnpike. I should infer from all I hear that he has got the steam up.

'You will readily guess with what feelings I have just made the discovery that my berth is in the same closet with those engaged by Professor Woodenscone, Mr. Slug, and Professor Grime. Professor Woodenscone has taken the shelf above me, and Mr. Slug and Professor Grime the two shelves opposite. Their luggage has already arrived. On Mr. Slug's bed is a long tin tube of about three inches in diameter, carefully closed at both ends. What can this contain? Some powerful instrument of a new construction, doubtless.

'*Ten minutes past nine.*

'Nobody has yet arrived, nor has anything fresh come in my way except several joints of beef and mutton, from which I conclude that a good plain dinner has been provided for tomorrow. There is a singular smell below, which gave me some uneasiness at first; but as the steward says it is always there, and never goes away, I am quite comfortable again. I learn from this man that the different sections will be distributed at the Black Boy and Stomach-ache, and the Boot-jack and Countenance. If this intelligence be true (and I have no reason to doubt it), your readers will draw such conclusions as their different opinions may suggest.

'I write down these remarks as they occur to me, or as the facts come to my knowledge, in order that my first impressions may lose nothing of their original vividness. I shall despatch them in small packets as opportunities arise.'

'*Half-past nine.*

'Some dark object has just appeared upon the wharf. I think it is a travelling carriage.'

'*A quarter to ten.*

'No, it isn't.'

'*Half-past ten.*

'The passengers are pouring in every instant. Four omnibuses full have just arrived upon the wharf, and all is bustle and activity. The noise and confusion are very great. Cloths are laid in the cabins, and the steward is placing blue plates-full of knobs of cheese at equal distances down the centre of the tables. He drops a great many knobs; but, being used to it, picks them up again with great dexterity, and, after wiping them on his sleeve, throws them back into the plates. He is a young man of exceedingly prepossessing appearance – either dirty or a mulatto, but I think the former.

'An interesting old gentleman, who came to the wharf in an omnibus, has just quarrelled violently with the porters, and is staggering towards the vessel with a large trunk in his arms. I trust and hope that he may reach it in safety; but the board he has to cross is narrow and slippery. Was that a splash? Gracious powers!

'I have just returned from the deck. The trunk is standing upon the extreme brink of the wharf, but the old gentleman is nowhere to be seen. The watchman is not sure whether he went down or not, but promises to drag for him the first thing tomorrow morning. May his humane efforts prove successful!

'Professor Nogo has this moment arrived with his nightcap on under his hat. He has ordered a glass of cold brandy and water, with a hard biscuit and a bason, and has gone straight to bed. What can this mean?

'The three other scientific gentlemen to whom I have already alluded have come on board, and have all tried their beds, with the exception of Professor Woodensconce, who sleeps in one of the top ones, and can't get into it. Mr. Slugg, who sleeps in the other top one, is unable to get out of his, and is to have his supper handed up by a boy. I have had the honour to introduce myself to these gentlemen, and we have amicably arranged the order in which we shall retire to rest; which it is necessary to agree upon, because, although the cabin in very comfortable, there is not room for more than one gentleman to be out of bed at a time, and even he must take his boots off in the passage.

'As I anticipated, the knobs of cheese were provided for the passengers' supper, and are now in course of consumption. Your readers will be surprised to hear that Professor Woodensconce has abstained from cheese for eight years, although he takes butter in considerable quantities. Professor Grime having lost several teeth, is unable, I observe, to eat his crusts without previously soaking them in his bottled porter. How interesting are these peculiarities!'

'Half-past eleven.

'Professors Woodensconce and Grime, with a degree of good humour that delights us all, have just arranged to toss for a bottle of mulled port. There has been some discussion whether the payment should be decided by the first toss or the best out of three. Eventually the latter course has been determined on. Deeply do I wish that both gentlemen could win; but that being impossible, I own that my personal aspirations (I speak as an individual, and do not compromise either you or your readers by this expression of feeling) are with Professor Woodensconce. I have backed that gentleman to the amount of eighteenpence.'

'*Twenty minutes to twelve.*

'Professor Grime has inadvertently tossed his half-crown out of one of the cabin-windows, and it has been arranged that the steward shall toss for him. Bets are offered on any side to any amount, but there are no takers.

'Professor Woodensconce has just called "woman," but the coin having lodged in a beam, is a long time coming down again. The interest and suspense of this one moment are beyond anything that can be imagined.'

'*Twelve o'clock.*

'The mulled port is smoking on the table before me, and Professor Grime has won. Tossing is a game of chance; but on every ground, whether of public or private character, intellectual endowments, or scientific attainments, I cannot help expressing my opinion that Professor Woodensconce *ought* to have come off victorious. There is an exultation about Professor Grime incompatible, I fear, with true greatness.'

'*A quarter past twelve.*

'Professor Grime continues to exult, and to boast of his victory in no very measured terms, observing that he always does win, and that he knew it would be a "head" beforehand, with many other remarks of a similar nature. Surely this gentleman is not so lost to every feeling of decency and propriety as not to feel and know the superiority of Professor Woodensconce? Is Professor Grime insane? or does he wish to be reminded in plain language of his true position in society, and the precise level of his acquirements and abilities? Professor Grime will do well to look to this.'

'*One o'clock.*

'I am writing in bed. The small cabin is illuminated by the feeble light of a flickering lamp suspended from the ceiling; Professor Grime is lying on the opposite shelf on the broad of his back, with his mouth wide open. The scene is indescribably solemn. The rippling of the tide, the noise of the sailors' feet overhead, the gruff voices on the river, the dogs on the shore, the snoring of the passengers, and a constant creaking of every plank in the vessel, are the only sounds that meet the ear. With these exceptions, all is profound silence.

'My curiosity has been within the last moment very much excited. Mr. Slug, who lies above Professor Grime, has cautiously withdrawn the curtains of his berth, and, after looking anxiously out, as if to satisfy himself that his companions are asleep, has taken up the tin tube of which I have before spoken, and is regarding it with great interest. What rare mechanical combination can be contained in that mysterious case? It is evidently a profound secret to all.'

'*A quarter past one.*

'The behaviour of Mr. Slug grows more and more mysterious. He has unscrewed the top of the tube, and now renews his observations upon his companions, evidently to make sure that he is wholly unobserved. He is clearly on the eve of some great experiment. Pray heaven that it be not a dangerous one; but the interests of science must be promoted, and I am prepared for the worst.'

'*Five minutes later.*

'He has produced a large pair of scissors, and drawn a roll of some substance, not unlike parchment in appearance, from the tin case. The experiment is about to begin. I must strain my eyes to the utmost, in the attempt to follow its minutest operation.'

'*Twenty minutes before two.*

'I have at length been enabled to ascertain that the tin tube contains a few yards of some celebrated plaster, recommended – as I discover on regarding the label attentively through my eye-glass – as a preservative against sea-sickness. Mr. Slug has cut it up into small portions, and is now sticking it over himself in every direction.'

'*Three o'clock.*

'Precisely a quarter of an hour ago we weighed anchor, and the machinery was suddenly put in motion with a noise so appalling, that Professor Woodensconce (who had ascended to his berth by means of a platform of carpet bags arranged by himself on geometrical principles) darted from his shelf head foremost, and, gaining his feet with all the rapidity of extreme terror, ran wildly into the ladies' cabin, under the impression that we were sinking, and uttering loud cries for aid. I am assured that the scene which ensued baffles all description. There were one hundred and forty-seven ladies in their respective berths at the time.

'Mr. Slug has remarked, as an additional instance of the extreme ingenuity of the steam-engine as applied to purposes of navigation, that in whatever part of the vessel a passenger's berth may be situated, the machinery always appears to be exactly under his pillow. He intends stating this very beautiful, though simple discovery, to the association.'

'*Half-past three.*

'We are still in smooth water; that is to say, in as smooth water as a steam-vessel ever can be, for, as Professor Woodensconce (who has just woke up) learnedly remarks, another great point of ingenuity about a steamer is, that it always carries a little storm with it. You can scarcely conceive how exciting the jerking pulsation of the ship becomes. It is a matter of positive difficulty to get to sleep.'

'*Friday afternoon, six o'clock.*

'I regret to inform you that Mr. Slug's plaster has proved of no avail. He is in great agony, but has applied several large, additional pieces notwithstanding. How affecting is this extreme devotion to science and pursuit of knowledge under the most trying circumstances!

'We were extremely happy this morning, and the breakfast was one of the most animated description. Nothing unpleasant occurred until noon, with the exception of Doctor Foxey's brown silk umbrella and white hat becoming entangled in the machinery while he was explaining to a knot of ladies the construction of the steam-engine. I fear the gravy soup for lunch was injudicious. We lost a great many passengers almost immediately afterwards.'

'*Half-past six.*

'I am again in bed. Anything so heartrending as Mr. Slug's sufferings it has never yet been my lot to witness.'

'*Seven o'clock.*

'A messenger has just come down for a clean pocket-handkerchief from Professor Woodensconce's bag, that unfortunate gentleman being quite unable to leave the deck, and imploring constantly to be thrown overboard. From this man I understand that Professor Nogo, though in a state of utter exhaustion, clings feebly to the hard biscuit and cold brandy and water, under the impression that they will yet restore him. Such is the triumph of mind over matter.

'Professor Grime is in bed, to all appearance quite well; but he *will* eat, and it is disagreeable to see him. Has this gentleman no sympathy with the sufferings of his fellow-creatures? If he has, on what principle can he call for mutton-chops – and smile?'

'*Black Boy and Stomach-ache,*
Oldcastle, Saturday noon.

'You will be happy to learn that I have at length arrived here in safety. The town is excessively crowded, and all the private lodgings and hotels are filled with *savants* of both sexes. The tremendous assemblage of intellect that one encounters in every street is in the last degree overwhelming.

'Notwithstanding the throng of people here, I have been fortunate enough to meet with very comfortable accommodation on very reasonable terms, having secured a sofa in the first-floor passage at one guinea per night, which includes permission to take my meals in the bar, on condition that I walk about the streets at all other times, to make room for other gentlemen similarly situated. I have been over the outhouses intended to be devoted to the reception of the various sections, both here and at the Boot-jack and Counte-nance, and am much delighted with the arrangements. Nothing can exceed the fresh appearance of the saw-dust with which the floors are sprinkled. The forms are of unplaned deal, and the general effect, as you can well imagine, is extremely beautiful.'

'*Half-past nine.*

'The number and rapidity of the arrivals are quite bewilder-ing. Within the last ten minutes a stage-coach has driven up to the door, filled inside and out with distinguished characters, comprising Mr. Muddlebranes, Mr. Drawley, Professor

Muff, Mr. X. Misty, Mr. X.X. Misty, Mr. Purblind, Professor Rummun, The Honourable and Reverend Mr. Long Eers, Professor John Ketch, Sir William Joltered, Doctor Buffer, Mr. Smith (of London), Mr. Brown (of Edinburgh), Sir Hookham Snivey, and Professor Pumpkinskull. The ten last-named gentlemen were wet through, and looked extremely intelligent.'

'*Sunday, two o'clock, p.m.*

'The Honourable and Reverend Mr. Long Eers, accompanied by Sir William Joltered, walked and drove this morning. They accomplished the former feat in boots, and the latter in a hired fly. This has naturally given rise to much discussion.

'I have just learnt that an interview has taken place at the Boot-jack and Countenance between Sowster, the active and intelligent beadle of this place, and Professor Pumpkinskull, who, as your readers are doubtless aware, is an influential member of the council. I forbear to communicate any of the rumours to which this very extraordinary proceeding has given rise until I have seen Sowster, and endeavoured to ascertain the truth from him.'

'*Half-past six.*

'I engaged a donkey-chaise shortly after writing the above, and proceeded at a brisk trot in the direction of Sowster's residence, passing through a beautiful expanse of country, with red brick buildings on either side, and stopping in the market-place to observe the spot where Mr. Kwakley's hat was blown off yesterday. It is an uneven piece of paving, but has certainly no appearance which would lead one to suppose that any such event had recently occurred there. From this point I proceeded – passing the gas-works and tallow-melter's – to a lane which had been pointed out to me as the beadle's place of residence; and before I had driven a dozen yards further, I had the good fortune to meet Sowster himself advancing towards me.

'Sowster is a fat man, with a more enlarged development of that peculiar conformation of countenance which is vulgarly termed a double chin that I remember to have ever seen before. He has also a very red nose, which he attributes to a habit of early rising – so red, indeed, that but for this explanation I should have supposed it to proceed from occasional inebriety. He informed me that he did not feel himself at liberty to relate what had passed between himself and professor Pumpkinskull, but had no objection to state that it was connected with a matter of police regulation, and added with peculiar significance "Never wos sitch times!"

'You will easily believe that this intelligence gave me considerable surprise, not wholly unmixed with anxiety, and that I lost no time in waiting on Professor Pumpkinskull, and stating the object of my visit. After a few moments' reflection, the Professor, who, I am bound to say, behaved with the utmost politeness, openly avowed (I mark the passage in italics) *that he had requested Sowster to attend on the Monday morning at the Boot-jack and Countenance, to keep off the boys; and that he had further desired that the under-beadle might be stationed, with the same object, at the Black Boy and Stomach-ache!*

'Now I leave this unconstitutional proceeding to your comments and the consideration of your readers. I have yet to learn that a beadle, without the precincts of a church, church-yard, or workhouse, and acting otherwise than under the express orders of churchwardens and overseers in council assembled, to enforce the law against people who come upon the parish, and other offenders, has any lawful authority whatever over the rising youth of this country. I have yet to learn that a beadle can be called out by any civilian to exercise a domination and despotism over the boys of Britain. I have yet to learn that a beadle will be permitted by the commission-ers of poor law regulation to wear out the soles and heels of his boots in illegal interference with the liberties of people not proved poor or otherwise criminal. I have yet to learn that a beadle has power to stop up the Queen's highway at his will and pleasure, or that the whole width of the street is not free and open to any man, boy, or woman in existence, up to the very walls of the houses – ay, be they Black Boys and Stomach-aches, or Boot-jacks and Countenances, I care not.'

'*Nine o'clock.*

'I have procured a local artist to make a faithful sketch of the tyrant Sowster, which, as he has acquired this infamous celebrity, you will no doubt wish to have engraved for the purpose of presenting a copy with every copy of your next number. I enclose it. The under-beadle has consented to write his life, but it is to be strictly anonymous.

'The accompanying likeness is of course from the life, and complete in every respect. Even if I had been totally ignorant of the man's real character, and it had been placed before me without remark, I should have shuddered involuntarily. There is an intense malignity of expression in the features, and a baleful ferocity of purpose in the ruffian's eye, which appals and sickens. His whole air is rampant with cruelty, nor is the stomach less characteristic of his demoniac propensities.'

'*Monday.*

'The great day has at length arrived. I have neither eyes, nor ears, nor pens, nor ink, nor paper, for anything but the wonderful proceedings that have astounded my senses. Let me collect my energies and proceed to the account.

'SECTION A. – ZOOLOGY AND BOTANY.

FRONT PARLOUR, BLACK BOY AND STOMACH-ACHE.

President – Sir William Joltered. *Vice-Presidents* – Mr. Muddlebranes and Mr. Drawley.

The Tyrant Sowster.

'Mr. X.X. Misty communicated some remarks on the disappearance of dancing bears from the streets of London, with observations on the exhibition of monkeys as connected with barrel-organs. The writer had observed, with feelings of the utmost pain and regret, that some years ago a sudden and unaccountable change in the public taste took place with reference to itinerant bears, who, being discountenanced by the populace, gradually fell off one by one from the streets of the metropolis, until not one remained to create a taste for natural history in the breasts of the poor and uninstructed. One bear, indeed, – a brown and ragged animal, – had lingered about the haunts of his former triumphs, with a worn and dejected visage and feeble limbs, and had essayed to wield his quarter-staff for the amusement of the multitude; but hunger, and an utter want of any due recompense for his abilities, had at length driven him from the field, and it was only too probable that he had fallen a sacrifice to the rising taste for grease. He regretted to add that a similar, and no less lamentable, change had taken place with reference to monkeys. These delightful animals had formerly been almost as plentiful as the organs on the tops of which they were accustomed to sit; the proportion in the year 1829 (it appeared by the parliamentary return) being as one monkey to three organs. Owing, however, to an altered taste in musical instruments, and the substitution, in a great measure, of narrow boxes of music for organs, which left the monkeys nothing to sit upon, this source of public amusement was wholly dried up. Considering it a matter of the deepest importance, in connection with national education, that the people should not lose such opportunities of making themselves acquainted with the manners and customs of two most interesting species of animals, the author submitted that some measures should be immediately taken for the restoration of these pleasing and truly intellectual amusements.

'The President inquired by what means the honourable member proposed to attain this most desirable end?

'The Author submitted that it could be most fully and satisfactorily accomplished, if Her Majesty's Government would cause to be brought over to England, and maintained at the public expense, and for the public amusement, such a number of bears as would enable every quarter of the town to be visited – say at least by three bears a week. No difficulty whatever need be experienced in providing a fitting place for the reception of these animals, as a commodious bear-garden could be erected in the immediate neighbourhood of both Houses of Parliament; obviously the most proper and eligible spot for such an establishment.

'Professor Mull doubted very much whether any correct ideas of natural history were propagated by the means to which the honourable member had so ably adverted. On the contrary, he believed that they had been the means of diffusing very incorrect and imperfect notions on the subject. He spoke from personal observation and personal experience, when he said that many children of great abilities had been induced to believe, from what they had observed in the streets, at and before the period to which the honourable gentleman had referred, that all monkeys were born in red coats and spangles, and that their hats and feathers also came by nature. He wished to know distinctly whether the honourable gentleman attributed the want of encouragement the bears had met with to the decline of public taste in that respect, or to a want of ability on the part of the bears themselves?

'Mr. X.X. Misty replied, that he could not bring himself to believe but that there must be a great deal of floating talent among the bears and monkeys generally; which, in the absence of any proper encouragement, was dispersed in other directions.

'Professor Pumpkinskull wished to take that opportunity of calling the attention of the section to a most important and serious point. The author of the treatise just read had alluded to the prevalent taste for bears'-grease as a means of promoting the growth of hair, which undoubtedly was diffused to a very great and (as it appeared to him) very alarming extent. No gentleman attending that section could fail to be aware of the fact that the youth of the present age evinced, by their behaviour in the streets, and at all places of public resort, a considerable lack of that gallantry and gentlemanly feeling which, in more ignorant times, had been thought becoming. He wished to know whether it were possible that a constant outward application of bears'-grease by the young gentlemen about town had imperceptibly infused into those unhappy persons something of the nature and quality of the bear. He shuddered as he threw out the remark; but if this theory, on inquiry, should prove to be well-founded, it would at once explain a great deal of unpleasant eccentricity of behaviour, which, without some such discovery, was wholly unaccountable.

'The President highly complimented the learned gentleman on his most valuable suggestion, which produced the greatest effect upon the assembly; and remarked that only a week previous he had seen some young gentlemen at a theatre eyeing a box of ladies with a fierce intensity, which nothing but the influence of some brutish appetite could possibly explain. It was dreadful to reflect that our youth were so rapidly verging into a generation of bears.

'After a scene of scientific enthusiasm it was resolved that this important question should be immediately submitted to the consideration of the council.

'The President wished to know whether any gentleman could inform the section what had become of the dancing-dogs?

'A Member replied, after some hesitation, that on the day after three glee-singers had been committed to prison as criminals by a late most zealous police-magistrate of the metropolis, the dogs had abandoned their professional duties, and dispersed themselves in different quarters of the town to gain a livelihood by less dangerous means. He was given to understand that since that period they had supported themselves by lying in wait for and robbing blind men's poodles.

'Mr. Flummery exhibited a twig, claiming to be a veritable branch of that noble tree known to naturalists as the SHAKS-PEARE, which has taken root in every land and climate, and gathered under the shade of its broad green boughs the great family of mankind. The learned gentleman remarked that the twig had been undoubtedly called by other names in its time; but that it had been pointed out to him by an old lady in Warwickshire, where the great tree had grown, as a shoot of the genuine SHAKSPEARE, by which name he begged to introduce it to his countrymen.

'The President wished to know what botanical definition the honourable gentleman could afford of the curiosity.

'Mr. Flummery expressed his opinion that it was A DECIDED PLANT.

'SECTION B. – DISPLAY OF MODELS AND MECHANICAL SCIENCE.

LARGE ROOM, BOOT-JACK AND COUNTENANCE.

President – Mr. Mallett. *Vice-Presidents* – Messrs. Leaver and Scroo.

'Mr. Crinkles exhibited a most beautiful and delicate machine, of little larger size than an ordinary snuff-box, manufactured entirely by himself, and composed exclusively of steel, by the aid of which more pockets could be picked in one hour than by the present slow and tedious process in four-and-twenty. The inventor remarked that it had been put into active operation in Fleet Street, the Strand, and other thoroughfares, and had never been once known to fail.

'After some slight delay, occasioned by the various members of the section buttoning their pockets.

'The President narrowly inspected the invention, and declared that he had never seen a machine of more beautiful or exquisite construction. Would the inventor be good enough to inform the section whether he had taken any and what means for bringing it into general operation?

'Mr. Crinkles stated that, after encountering some preliminary difficulties, he had succeeded in putting himself in communication with Mr. Fogle Hunter, and other gentlemen connected with the swell mob, who had awarded the invention the very highest and most unqualified approbation. He regretted to say, however, that these distinguished practitioners, in common with a gentleman of the name of Gimlet-eyed Tommy, and other members of a secondary grade of the profession whom he was understood to represent, entertained an insuperable objection to its being brought into general use, on the ground that it would have the inevitable effect of almost entirely superseding manual labour, and throwing a great number of highly-deserving persons out of employment.

'The President hoped that no such fanciful objections would be allowed to stand in the way of such a great public improvement.

'Mr. Crinkles hoped so too; but he feared that if the gentlemen of the swell mob persevered in their objection, nothing could be done.

'Professor Grime suggested, that surely, in that case, Her Majesty's government might be prevailed upon to take it up.

'Mr. Crinkles said, that if the objection were found to be insuperable he should apply to parliament, which he thought could not fail to recognise the utility of the invention.

'The President observed that, up to this time parliament had certainly got on very well without it; but, as they did their business on a very large scale, he had no doubt they would gladly adopt the improvement. His only fear was that the machine might be worn out by constant working.

'Mr. Coppernose called the attention of the section to a proposition of great magnitude and interest, illustrated by a vast number of models, and stated with much clearness and perspicuity in a treatise entitled "Practical Suggestions on the necessity of providing some harmless and wholesome relaxation for the young noblemen of England." His proposition was, that a space of ground of not less than ten miles in length and four in breadth should be purchased by a new company, to be incorporated by Act of Parliament, and inclosed by a brick wall of not less than twelve feet in height. He proposed that it should be laid out with highway roads, turnpikes, bridges, miniature villages, and every object that could conduce to the comfort and glory of Four-in-hand Clubs, so that they might be fairly presumed to require no drive beyond it. This delightful retreat would be fitted up with most commodious and extensive stables, for the convenience of such of the nobility and gentry as had a taste for ostlering, and with houses of entertainment furnished in the most expensive and handsome style. It would be further provided with whole streets of door-knockers and bell-handles of extra size, so constructed that they could be easily wrenched off at night, and regularly screwed on again, by attendants provided for the purpose, every day. There would also be gas lamps of real glass, which could be broken at a comparatively small expense per dozen, and a broad and handsome foot pavement for gentlemen to drive their cabriolets upon when they were humorously disposed – for the full enjoyment of which feat live pedestrians would be procured from the workhouse at a very small charge per head. The place being inclosed, and carefully screened from the intrusion of the public, there would be no objection to gentlemen laying aside any article of their costume that was considered to interfere with a pleasant frolic, or, indeed, to their walking about without any costume at all, if they liked that better. In short, every facility of enjoyment would be afforded that the most gentlemanly person could possibly desire. But as even these advantages would be incomplete unless there were some means provided of enabling the nobility and gentry to display their prowess when they sallied forth after dinner, and as some inconvenience might be experienced in the event of their being reduced to the necessity of pummelling each other, the inventor had turned his attention to the construction of an entirely new police force, composed exclusively of automaton figures, which, with the assistance of the ingenious Signor Gagliardi, of Windmill-street, in the Haymarket, he had succeeded in making with such nicety, that a policeman, cab-driver, or old woman, made upon the principle of the models exhibited, would walk about until knocked down like any real man; nay, more, if set upon and beaten by six or eight noblemen or gentlemen, after it was down, the figure would utter divers groans, mingled with entreaties for mercy, thus rendering the illusion complete, and the enjoyment perfect. But the invention did not stop even here; for station-houses would be built, containing good beds for noblemen and gentlemen during the night, and in the morning they would repair to a commodious police office, where a pantomimic investigation would take place before the automaton magistrates, – quite equal to life, – who would fine them in so many counters, with which they would be previously provided for the purpose. This office would be furnished with an inclined plane, for the convenience of any nobleman or gentleman who might wish to bring in his horse as a witness; and the prisoners would be at perfect liberty, as they were now, to interrupt the complainants as much as they pleased, and to make any remarks that they thought proper. The charge for these amusements would amount to very little more than they already cost, and the inventor submitted that the public would be much benefited and comforted by the proposed arrangement.

'Professor Nogo wished to be informed what amount of automaton police force it was proposed to raise in the first instance.

'Mr. Coppernose replied, that it was proposed to begin with seven divisions of police of a score each, lettered from A to G inclusive. It was proposed that not more than half this number should be placed on active duty, and that the remainder should be kept on shelves in the police office ready to be called out at a moment's notice.

'The President, awarding the utmost merit to the ingenious gentleman who had originated the idea, doubted whether the automaton police would quite answer the purpose. He feared that noblemen and gentlemen would perhaps require the excitement of threshing living subjects.

'Mr. Coppernose submitted, that as the usual odds in such cases were ten noblemen or gentlemen to one policeman or cab-driver, it could make very little difference in point of excitement whether the policeman or cab-driver were a man or a block. The great advantage would be, that a policeman's limbs might be all knocked off, and yet he would be in a condition to do duty next day. He might even give his evidence next morning with his head in his hand, and give it equally well.

'Professor Muff. – Will you allow me to ask you, sir, of what materials it is intended that the magistrates' heads shall be composed?

'Mr. Coppernose. – The magistrates will have wooden heads of course, and they will be made of the toughest and thickest materials that can possibly be obtained.

'Professor Muff. – I am quite satisfied. This is a great invention.

'Professor Nogo. – I see but one objection to it. It appears to me that the magistrates ought to talk.

'Mr. Coppernose no sooner heard this suggestion than he touched a small spring in each of the two models of magistrates which were placed upon the table; one of the figures immediately began to exclaim with great volubility that he was sorry to see gentlemen in such a situation, and the other to express a fear that the policeman was intoxicated.

'The section, as with one accord, declared with a shout of applause that the invention was complete; and the President, much excited, retired with Mr. Coppernose to lay it before the council. On his return,

'Mr. Tickle displayed his newly-invented spectacles, which enabled the wearer to discern, in very bright colours, objects at a great distance, and rendered him wholly blind to those immediately before him. It was, he said, a most valuable and useful invention, based strictly upon the principle of the human eye.

'The President required some information upon this point. He had yet to learn that the human eye was remarkable for the peculiarities of which the honourable gentleman had spoken.

'Mr. Tickle was rather astonished to hear this, when the President could not fail to be aware that a large number of most excellent persons and great statesmen could see, with the naked eye, most marvellous horrors on West India plantations, while they could discern nothing whatever in the interior of Manchester cotton mills. He must know, too, with what quickness of perception most people could discover their neighbour's faults, and how very blind they were to their own. If the President differed from the great majority of men in this respect, his eye was a defective one, and it was to assist his vision that these glasses were made.

'Mr. Blank exhibited a model of a fashionable annual, composed of copperplates, gold leaf, and silk boards, and worked entirely by milk and water.

'Mr. Prosee, after examining the machine, declared it to be so ingeniously composed, that he was wholly unable to discover how it went on at all.

'Mr. Blank. – Nobody can, and that is the beauty of it.

'SECTION C. – ANATOMY AND MEDICINE.

BAR ROOM, BLACK BOY AND STOMACH-ACHE.

President – Dr. Soemup. *Vice-Presidents* – Messrs. Pessell
and Mortair.

'Dr. Grummidge stated to the section a most interesting
case of monomania, and described the course of treatment he
had pursued with perfect success. The patient was a married
lady in the middle rank of life, who, having seen another lady
at an evening party in a full suit of pearls, was suddenly seized
with a desire to possess a similar equipment, although her
husband's finances were by no means equal to the necessary
outlay. Finding her wish ungratified, she fell sick, and the
symptoms soon became so alarming, that he (Dr. Grummidge) was called in. At this period the prominent tokens of
the disorder were sullenness, a total indisposition to perform
domestic duties, great peevishness, and extreme languor,
except when pearls were mentioned, at which times the pulse
quickened, the eyes grew brighter, the pupils dilated, and the
patient, after various incoherent exclamations, burst into a
passion of tears, and exclaimed that nobody cared for her, and
that she wished herself dead. Finding that the patient's appetite
was affected in the presence of company, he began by
ordering a total abstinence from all stimulants, and forbidding
any sustenance but weak gruel; he then took twenty ounces of
blood, applied a blister under each ear, one upon the chest,
and another on the back; having done which, and administered five grains of calomel, he left the patient to her repose.
The next day she was somewhat low, but decidedly better,
and all appearances of irritation were removed. The next day
she improved still further, and on the next again. On the
fourth there was some appearance of a return of the old

symptoms, which no sooner developed themselves, than he administered another dose of calomel, and left strict orders that, unless a decidedly favourable change occurred within two hours, the patient's head should be immediately shaved to the very last curl. From that moment she began to mend, and, in less than four-and-twenty hours was perfectly restored. She did not now betray the least emotion at the sight or mention of pearls or any other ornaments. She was cheerful and good-humoured, and a most beneficial change had been effected in her whole temperament and condition.

'Mr. Pipkin (M.R.C.S.) read a short but most interesting communication in which he sought to prove the complete belief of Sir William Courtenay, otherwise Thom, recently shot at Canterbury, in the Homoeopathic system. The section would bear in mind that one of the Homoeopathic doctrines was, that infinitesimal doses of any medicine which would occasion the disease under which the patient laboured, supposing him to be in a healthy state, would cure it. Now, it was a remarkable circumstance – proved in the evidence – that the deceased Thom employed a woman to follow him about all day with a pail of water, assuring her that one drop (a purely homoeopathic remedy, the section would observe), placed upon his tongue, after death, would restore him. What was the obvious inference? That Thom, who was marching and countermarching in osier beds, and other swampy places, was impressed with a presentiment that he should be drowned; in which case, had his instructions been complied with, he could not fail to have been brought to life again instantly by his own prescription. As it was, if this woman, or any other person, had administered an infinitesimal dose of lead and gunpowder immediately after he fell, he would have recovered forthwith. But unhappily the woman concerned did not possess the power of reasoning by analogy, or carrying out a principle, and thus the unfortunate gentleman had been sacrificed to the ignorance of the peasantry.

'SECTION D. – STATISTICS.

OUT-HOUSE, BLACK BOY AND STOMACH-ACHE.

President – Mr. Slug. *Vice-Presidents* – Messrs. Noakes and Styles.

'Mr. Kwakley stated the result of some most ingenious statistical inquiries relative to the difference between the value of the qualification of several members of Parliament as published to the world, and its real nature and amount. After reminding the section that every member of Parliament for a town or borough was supposed to possess a clear freehold estate of three hundred pounds per annum, the honourable gentleman excited great amusement and laughter by stating the exact amount of freehold property possessed by a column of legislators, in which he had included himself. It appeared from this table, that the amount of such income possessed by each was 0 pounds, 0 shillings, and 0 pence, yielding an average of the same. (Great laughter.) It was pretty well known that there were accommodating gentlemen in the habit of furnishing new members with temporary qualifications, to the ownership of which they swore solemnly – of course as a mere matter of form. He argued from these *data* that it was wholly unnecessary for members of Parliament to possess any property at all, especially as when they had none the public could get them so much cheaper.

'SUPPLEMENTARY SECTION, E. – UMBUGOLOGY AND DITCHWATERISICS.

President – Mr. Grub. *Vice-Presidents* – Messrs. Dull and Dummy.

'A paper was read by the secretary descriptive of a bay pony with one eye, which had been seen by the author standing in a butcher's cart at the corner of Newgate Market. The communication described the author of the paper as having, in the prosecution of a mercantile pursuit, betaken himself one Saturday morning last summer from Somers Town to Cheapside; in the course of which expedition he had beheld the extraordinary appearance above described. The pony had one distinct eye, and it had been pointed out to him by his friend Captain Blunderbore, of the Horse Marines, who assisted the author in his search, that whenever he winked this eye he whisked his tail (possibly to drive the flies off), but that he always winked and whisked at the same time. The animal was lean, spavined, and tottering; and the author proposed to constitute it of the family of *Fitfordogsmeataurious*. It certainly did occur to him that there was no case on record of a pony with one clearly-defined and distinct organ of vision, winking and whisking at the same moment.

'Mr. Q.J. Snuffletoffle had heard of a pony winking his eye, and likewise of a pony whisking his tail, but whether they were two ponies or the same pony he could not undertake positively to say. At all events, he was acquainted with no authenticated instance of a simultaneous winking and whisking, and he really could not but doubt the existence of such a marvellous pony in opposition to all those natural laws by which ponies were governed. Referring, however, to the mere question of his one organ of vision, might he suggest the possibility of this pony having been literally half asleep at the time he was seen, and having closed only one eye.

'The President observed that, whether the pony was half asleep or fast asleep, there could be no doubt that the association was wide awake, and therefore that they had better get the business over, and go to dinner. He had certainly never seen anything analogous to this pony, but he was not prepared to doubt its existence; for he had seen many queerer ponies in his time, though he did not pretend to have seen any more remarkable donkeys than the other gentlemen around him.

'Professor John Ketch was then called upon to exhibit the skull of the late Mr. Greenacre, which he produced from a blue bag, remarking, on being invited to make any observations that occurred to him, "that he'd pound it as that 'ere 'spectable section had never seed a more gamerer cove nor he vos."

'A most animated discussion upon this interesting relic ensued; and, some difference of opinion arising respecting the real character of the deceased gentleman, Mr. Blubb delivered a lecture upon the cranium before him, clearly showing that Mr. Greenacre possessed the organ of destructiveness to a most unusual extent, with a most remarkable development of the organ of carveativeness. Sir Hookham Snivey was proceeding to combat this opinion, when Professor Ketch suddenly interrupted the proceedings by exclaiming, with great excitement of manner, "Walker!"

'The President begged to call the learned gentleman to order.

'Professor Ketch. "Order be blowed! you've got the wrong un, I tell you. It ain't no e'd at all; it's a coker-nut as my brother-in-law has been a-carvin', to hornament his new baked tatur-stall wots a-comin' down 'ere vile the 'sociation's in the town. Hand over, vill you?"

'With these words, Professor Ketch hastily repossessed himself of the cocoa-nut, and drew forth the skull, in mistake for which he had exhibited it. A most interesting conversation ensued; but as there appeared some doubt ultimately whether the skull was Mr. Greenacre's, or a hospital patient's, or a pauper's, or a man's, or a woman's, or a monkey's, no particular result was obtained.'

'I cannot,' says our talented correspondent in conclusion, 'I cannot close my account of these gigantic researches and sublime and noble triumphs without repeating a *bon mot* of Professor Woodensconce's, which shows how the greatest minds may occasionally unbend when truth can be presented to listening ears, clothed in an attractive and playful form. I was standing by, when, after a week of feasting and feeding, that learned gentleman, accompanied by the whole body of wonderful men, entered the hall yesterday, where a sumptuous dinner was prepared; where the richest wines sparkled on the board, and fat bucks – propitiatory sacrifices to learning – sent forth their savoury odours. "Ah!" said Professor Woodensconce, rubbing his hands, "this is what we meet for; this is what inspires us; this is what keeps us together, and beckons us onward; this is the *spread* of science, and a glorious spread it is."'

THE PANTOMIME OF LIFE

Before we plunge headlong into this paper, let us at once confess to a fondness for pantomimes – to a gentle sympathy with clowns and pantaloons – to an unqualified admiration of harlequins and columbines – to a chaste delight in every action of their brief existence, varied and many-coloured as those actions are, and inconsistent though they occasionally be with those rigid and formal rules of propriety which regulate the proceedings of meaner and less comprehensive minds. We revel in pantomimes – not because they dazzle one's eyes with tinsel and gold leaf; not because they present to us, once again, the well-beloved chalked faces, and goggle eyes of our childhood; not even because, like Christmas-day, and Twelfth-night, and Shrove-Tuesday, and one's own birthday, they come to us but once a year; – our attachment is founded on a graver and a very different reason. A pantomime is to us, a mirror of life; nay more, we maintain that it is so to audiences generally, although they are not aware of it, and that this very circumstance is the secret cause of their amusement and delight.

Let us take a slight example. The scene is a street: an elderly gentleman, with a large face and strongly marked features, appears. His countenance beams with a sunny smile, and a perpetual dimple is on his broad, red cheek. He is evidently an opulent elderly gentleman, comfortable in circumstances, and well-to-do in the world. He is not unmindful of the adornment of his person, for he is richly, not to say gaudily, dressed; and that he indulges to a reasonable extent in the pleasures of the table may be inferred from the joyous and oily manner in which he rubs his stomach, by way of informing the audience that he is going home to dinner. In the fulness of his heart, in the fancied security of wealth, in the possession and enjoyment of all the good things of life, the elderly gentleman suddenly loses his footing, and stumbles. How the audience roar! He is set upon by a noisy and officious crowd, who buffet and cuff him unmercifully. They scream with delight! Every time the elderly gentleman struggles to get up, his relentless persecutors knock him down again. The spectators are convulsed with merriment! And when at last the elderly gentleman does get up, and staggers away, despoiled of hat, wig, and clothing, himself battered to pieces, and his watch and money gone, they are exhausted with laughter, and express their merriment and admiration in rounds of applause.

Is this like life? Change the scene to any real street; – to the Stock Exchange, or the City banker's; the merchant's counting-house, or even the tradesman's shop. See any one of these men fall, – the more suddenly, and the nearer the zenith of his pride and riches, the better. What a wild hallo is raised over his prostrate carcase by the shouting mob; how they whoop and yell as he lies humbled beneath them! Mark how eagerly they set upon him when he is down; and how they mock and deride him as he slinks away. Why, it is the pantomime to the very letter.

'Of all the pantomimic *dramatis personae*, we consider the pantaloon the most worthless and debauched. Independent of the dislike one naturally feels at seeing a gentleman of his years engaged in pursuits highly unbecoming his gravity and time of life, we cannot conceal from ourselves the fact that he is a treacherous, worldly-minded old villain, constantly enticing his younger companion, the clown, into acts of fraud or petty larceny, and generally standing aside to watch the result of the enterprise. If it be successful, he never forgets to return for his share of the spoil; but if it turn out a failure, he generally retires with remarkable caution and expedition, and keeps carefully aloof until the affair has blown over. His amorous propensities, too, are eminently disagreeable; and his mode of addressing ladies in the open street at noon-day is downright improper, being usually neither more nor less than a perceptible tickling of the aforesaid ladies in the waist, after committing which, he starts back, manifestly ashamed (as well he may be) of his own indecorum and temerity; continuing, nevertheless, to ogle and beckon to them from a distance in a very unpleasant and immoral manner.

Is there any man who cannot count a dozen pantaloons in his own social circle? Is there any man who has not seen them swarming at the west end of the town on a sunshiny day or a summer's evening, going through the last-named pantomimic feats with as much liquorish energy, and as total an absence of reserve, as if they were on the very stage itself? We can tell upon our fingers a dozen pantaloons of our acquaintance at this moment – capital pantaloons, who have been performing all kinds of strange freaks, to the great amusement of their friends and acquaintances, for years past; and who to this day are making such comical and ineffectual attempts to be young and dissolute, that all beholders are like to die with laughter.

Take that old gentleman who has just emerged from the *Cafe de l'Europe* in the Haymarket, where he has been dining at the expense of the young man upon town with whom he shakes hands as they part at the door of the tavern. The affected warmth of that shake of the hand, the courteous nod, the obvious recollection of the dinner, the savoury flavour of which still hangs upon his lips, are all characteristics of his great prototype. He hobbles away humming an opera tune, and twirling his cane to and fro, with affected carelessness. Suddenly he stops – 'tis at the milliner's window. He peeps through one of the large panes of glass; and, his view of the ladies within being obstructed by the India shawls, directs his attentions to the young girl with the band-box in her hand, who is gazing in at the window also. See! He draws beside her. He coughs; she turns away from him. He draws near her again; she disregards him. He gleefully chucks her under the chin, and, retreating a few steps, nods and beckons with fantastic grimaces, while the girl bestows a contemptuous and supercilious look upon his wrinkled visage. She turns away with a flounce, and the old gentleman trots after her with a toothless chuckle. The pantaloon to the life!

But the close resemblance which the clowns of the stage bear to those of everyday life is perfectly extraordinary. Some people talk with a sigh of the decline of pantomime, and murmur in low and dismal tones the name of Grimaldi. We mean no disparagement to the worthy and excellent old man when we say that this is downright nonsense. Clowns that beat Grimaldi all to nothing turn up every day, and nobody patronizes them – more's the pity!

'I know who you mean,' says some dirty-faced patron of Mr. Osbaldistone's, laying down the Miscellany when he has got thus far, and bestowing upon vacancy a most knowing glance; 'you mean C.J. Smith as did Guy Fawkes, and George Barnwell at the Garden.' The dirty-faced gentleman has hardly uttered the words, when he is interrupted by a young gentleman in no shirt-collar and a Petersham coat. 'No, no,' says the young gentleman; 'he means Brown, King, and Gibson, at the 'Delphi.' Now, with great deference both to the first-named gentleman with the dirty face, and the last-named gentleman in the non-existing shirt-collar, we do *not* mean either the performer who so grotesquely burlesqued the Popish conspirator, or the three unchangeables who have been dancing the same dance under different imposing titles, and doing the same thing under various high-sounding names for some five or six years last past. We have no sooner made this avowal, than the public, who have hitherto been silent witnesses of the dispute, inquire what on earth it is we *do* mean; and, with becoming respect, we proceed to tell them.

It is very well known to all playgoers and pantomime-seers, that the scenes in which a theatrical clown is at the very height of his glory are those which are described in the play-bills as 'Cheesemonger's shop and Crockery warehouse,' or 'Tailor's shop, and Mrs. Queertable's boarding-house,' or places bearing some such title, where the great fun of the thing consists in the hero's taking lodgings which he has not the slightest intention of paying for, or obtaining goods under false pretences, or abstracting the stock-in-trade of the respectable shop-keeper next door, or robbing warehouse porters as they pass under his window, or, to shorten the catalogue, in his swindling everybody he possibly can, it only remaining to be observed that, the more extensive the swindling is, and the more barefaced the impudence of the swindler, the greater the rapture and ecstasy of the audience. Now it is a most remarkable fact that precisely this sort of thing occurs in real life day after day, and nobody sees the humour of it. Let us illustrate our position by detailing the plot of this portion of the pantomime – not of the theatre, but of life.

The Honourable Captain Fitz-Whisker Fiercy, attended by his livery servant Do'em – a most respectable servant to look at, who has grown grey in the service of the captain's family – views, treats for, and ultimately obtains possession of, the unfurnished house, such a number, such a street. All the tradesmen in the neighbourhood are in agonies of competition for the captain's custom; the captain is a good-natured, kind-hearted, easy man, and, to avoid being the cause of disappointment to any, he most handsomely gives orders to all. Hampers of wine, baskets of provisions, cart-loads of furniture, boxes of jewellery, supplies of luxuries of the costliest description, flock to the house of the Honourable Captain Fitz-Whisker Fiercy, where they are received with the utmost readiness by the highly respectable Do'em; while the captain himself struts and swaggers about with that compound air of conscious superiority and general blood-thirstiness which a military captain should always, and does most times, wear, to the admiration and terror of plebeian men. But the tradesmen's backs are no sooner turned, than the captain, with all the eccentricity of a mighty mind, and assisted by the faithful Do'em, whose devoted fidelity is not the least touching part of his character, disposes of everything to great advantage; for, although the articles fetch small sums, still they are sold considerably above cost price, the cost to the captain having been nothing at all. After various manoeuvres, the imposture is discovered, Fitz-Fiercy and Do'em are recognized as confederates, and the police office to which they are both taken is thronged with their dupes.

Who can fail to recognise in this, the exact counterpart of the best portion of a theatrical pantomime – Fitz-Whisker Fiercy by the clown; Do'em by the pantaloon; and supernumeraries by the tradesmen? The best of the joke, too, is, that the very coal-merchant who is loudest in his complaints against the person who defrauded him, is the identical man who sat in the centre of the very front row of the pit last night and laughed the most boisterously at this very same thing, – and not so well done either. Talk of Grimaldi, we say again! Did Grimaldi, in his best days, ever do anything in this way equal to Da Costa?

The mention of this latter justly celebrated clown reminds us of his last piece of humour, the fraudulently obtaining certain stamped acceptances from a young gentleman in the army. We had scarcely laid down our pen to contemplate for a few moments this admirable actor's performance of that exquisite practical joke, than a new branch of our subject flashed suddenly upon us. So we take it up again at once.

All people who have been behind the scenes, and most people who have been before them, know, that in the representation of a pantomime, a good many men are sent upon the stage for the express purpose of being cheated, or knocked down, or both. Now, down to a moment ago, we

had never been able to understand for what possible purpose a
great number of odd, lazy, large-headed men, whom one is in
the habit of meeting here, and there, and everywhere, could
ever have been created. We see it all, now. They are the
supernumeraries in the pantomime of life; the men who have
been thrust into it, with no other view than to be constantly
tumbling over each other, and running their heads against all
sorts of strange things. We sat opposite to one of these men at
a supper-table, only last week. Now we think of it, he was
exactly like the gentlemen with the pasteboard heads and
faces, who do the corresponding business in the theatrical
pantomimes; there was the same broad stolid simper – the
same dull leaden eye – the same unmeaning, vacant stare; and
whatever was said, or whatever was done, he always came in
at precisely the wrong place, or jostled against something that
he had not the slightest business with. We looked at the man
across the table again and again; and could not satisfy
ourselves what race of beings to class him with. How very
odd that this never occurred to us before!

We will frankly own that we have been much troubled with
the harlequin. We see harlequins of so many kinds in the real
living pantomime, that we hardly know which to select as the
proper fellow of him of the theatres. At one time we were
disposed to think that the harlequin was neither more nor less
than a young man of family and independent property, who
had run away with an opera dancer, and was fooling his life
and his means away in light and trivial amusements. On
reflection, however, we remembered that harlequins are occasionally guilty of witty, and even clever acts, and we are rather
disposed to acquit our young men of family and independent
property, generally speaking, of any such misdemeanours.
On a more mature consideration of the subject, we have
arrived at the conclusion that the harlequins of life are just
ordinary men, to be found in no particular walk or degree, on
whom a certain station, or particular conjunction of circum-

stances, confers the magic wand. And this brings us to a few words on the pantomime of public and political life, which we shall say at once, and then conclude – merely premising in this place that we decline any reference whatever to the columbine, being in no wise satisfied of the nature of her connection with her parti-coloured lover, and not feeling by any means clear that we should be justified in introducing her to the virtuous and respectable ladies who peruse our lucubrations.

We take it that the commencement of a Session of Parliament is neither more nor less than the drawing up of the curtain for a grand comic pantomime, and that his Majesty's most gracious speech on the opening thereof may be not inaptly compared to the clown's opening speech of 'Here we are!' 'My lords and gentlemen, here we are!' appears, to our mind at least, to be a very good abstract of the point and meaning of the propitiatory address of the ministry. When we remember how frequently this speech is made, immediately after *the change* too, the parallel is quite perfect, and still more singular.

Perhaps the cast of our political pantomime never was richer than at this day. We are particularly strong in clowns. At no former time, we should say, have we had such astonishing tumblers, or performers so ready to go through the whole of their feats for the amusement of an admiring throng. Their extreme readiness to exhibit, indeed, has given rise to some ill-natured reflections; it having been objected that by exhibiting gratuitously through the country when the theatre is closed, they reduce themselves to the level of mountebanks, and thereby tend to degrade the respectability of the profession. Certainly Grimaldi never did this sort of thing; and though Brown, King, and Gibson have gone to the Surrey in vacation time, and Mr. C.J. Smith has ruralised at Sadler's Wells, we find no theatrical precedent for a general tumbling through the country, except in the gentleman, name unknown, who threw summersets on behalf of the late Mr.

Richardson, and who is no authority either, because he had never been on the regular boards.

But, laying aside this question, which after all is a mere matter of taste, we may reflect with pride and gratification of heart on the proficiency of our clowns as exhibited in the season. Night after night will they twist and tumble about, till two, three, and four o'clock in the morning; playing the strangest antics, and giving each other the funniest slaps on the face that can possibly be imagined, without evincing the smallest tokens of fatigue. The strange noises, the confusion, the shouting and roaring, amid which all this is done, too, would put to shame the most turbulent sixpenny gallery that ever yelled through a boxing-night.

It is especially curious to behold one of these clowns compelled to go through the most surprising contortions by the irresistible influence of the wand of office, which his leader or harlequin holds above his head. Acted upon by this wonderful charm he will become perfectly motionless, moving neither hand, foot, nor finger, and will even lose the faculty of speech at an instant's notice; or on the other hand, he will become all life and animation if required, pouring forth a torrent of words without sense or meaning, throwing himself into the wildest and most fantastic contortions, and even grovelling on the earth and licking up the dust. These exhibitions are more curious than pleasing; indeed, they are rather disgusting than otherwise, except to the admirers of such things, with whom we confess we have no fellow-feeling.

Strange tricks – very strange tricks – are also performed by the harlequin who holds for the time being the magic wand which we have just mentioned. The mere waving it before a man's eyes will dispossess his brains of all the notions previously stored there, and fill it with an entirely new set of ideas; one gentle tap on the back will alter the colour of a man's coat completely; and there are some expert performers, who, having this wand held first on one side and then on the other, will change from side to side, turning their coats at every evolution, with so much rapidity and dexterity, that the quickest eye can scarcely detect their motions. Occasionally, the genius who confers the wand, wrests it from the hand of the temporary possessor, and consigns it to some new performer; on which occasions all the characters change sides, and then the race and the hard knocks begin anew.

We might have extended this chapter to a much greater length – we might have carried the comparison into the liberal professions – we might have shown, as was in fact our original purpose, that each is in itself a little pantomime with scenes and characters of its own, complete; but, as we fear we have been quite lengthy enough already, we shall leave this chapter just where it is. A gentleman, not altogether unknown as a dramatic poet, wrote thus a year or two ago –

'All the world's a stage,
And all the men and women merely players:'

and we, tracking out his footsteps at the scarcely-worth-mentioning little distance of a few millions of leagues behind, venture to add, by way of new reading, that he meant a Pantomime, and that we are all actors in The Pantomime of Life.

SOME PARTICULARS CONCERNING
A LION

We have a great respect for lions in the abstract. In common with most other people, we have heard and read of many instances of their bravery and generosity. We have duly admired that heroic self-denial and charming philanthropy which prompts them never to eat people except when they are hungry, and we have been deeply impressed with a becoming sense of the politeness they are said to display towards unmarried ladies of a certain state. All natural histories teem with anecdotes illustrative of their excellent qualities; and one old spelling book in particular recounts a touching instance of an old lion, of high moral dignity and stern principle, who felt it his imperative duty to devour a young man who had contracted a habit of swearing, as a striking example to the rising generation.

All this is extremely pleasant to reflect upon, and, indeed, says a very great deal in favour of lions as a mass. We are bound to state, however, that such individual lions as we have happened to fall in with have not put forth any very striking characteristics, and have not acted up to the chivalrous character assigned them by their chroniclers. We never saw a lion in what is called his natural state, certainly; that is to say, we have never met a lion out walking in a forest, or crouching in his lair under a tropical sun, waiting till his dinner should happen to come by, hot from the baker's. But we have seen some under the influence of captivity, and the pressure of misfortune; and we must say that they appeared to us very apathetic, heavy-headed fellows.

The lion at the Zoological Gardens, for instance. He is all very well; he has an undeniable mane, and looks very fierce; but, Lord bless us! what of that? The lions of the fashionable world look just as ferocious, and are the most harmless creatures breathing. A box-lobby lion or a Regent-street animal will put on a most terrible aspect, and roar fearfully, if you affront him; but he will never bite, and, if you offer to attack him manfully, will fairly turn tail and sneak off. Doubtless these creatures roam about sometimes in herds, and, if they meet any especially meek-looking and peaceably-disposed fellow, will endeavour to frighten him; but the faintest show of a vigorous resistance is sufficient to scare them even then. These are pleasant characteristics, whereas we make it a matter of distinct charge against the Zoological lion and his brethren at the fairs, that they are sleepy, dreamy, sluggish quadrupeds.

We do not remember to have ever seen one of them perfectly awake, except at feeding-time. In every respect we uphold the biped lions against their four-footed namesakes, and we boldly challenge controversy upon the subject.

With these opinions it may be easily imagined that our curiosity and interest were very much excited the other day, when a lady of our acquaintance called on us and resolutely declined to accept our refusal of her invitation to an evening party; 'for,' said she, 'I have got a lion coming.' We at once retracted our plea of a prior engagement, and became as anxious to go, as we had previously been to stay away.

We went early, and posted ourselves in an eligible part of the drawing-room, from whence we could hope to obtain a full view of the interesting animal. Two or three hours passed, the quadrilles began, the room filled; but no lion appeared. The lady of the house became inconsolable, – for it is one of the peculiar privileges of these lions to make solemn appointments and never keep them, – when all of a sudden there came a tremendous double rap at the street door, and the master of

the house, after gliding out (unobserved as he flattered himself) to peep over the banisters, came into the room, rubbing
his hands together with great glee, and cried out in a very
important voice, 'My dear, Mr. —— (naming the lion) has
this moment arrived.'

Upon this, all eyes were turned towards the door, and we
observed several young ladies, who had been laughing and
conversing previously with great gaiety and good humour,
grow extremely quiet and sentimental; while some young
gentlemen, who had been cutting great figures in the facetious
and small-talk way, suddenly sank very obviously in the
estimation of the company, and were looked upon with great
coldness and indifference. Even the young man who had been
ordered from the music shop to play the pianoforte was
visibly affected, and struck several false notes in the excess of
his excitement.

All this time there was a great talking outside, more than
once accompanied by a loud laugh, and a cry of 'Oh! capital!
excellent!' from which we inferred that the lion was jocose,
and that these exclamations were occasioned by the transports
of his keeper and our host. Nor were we deceived; for when
the lion at last appeared, we overheard his keeper, who was a
little prim man, whisper to several gentlemen of his acquaintance, with uplifted hands, and every expression of half-
suppressed admiration, that —— (naming the lion again) was
in *such* cue tonight!

The lion was a literary one. Of course, there were a vast
number of people present who had admired his roarings,
and were anxious to be introduced to him; and very
pleasant it was to see them brought up for the purpose, and
to observe the patient dignity with which he received all
their patting and caressing. This brought forcibly to our
mind what we had so often witnessed at country fairs,
where the other lions are compelled to go through as many
forms of courtesy as they chance to be acquainted with,

just as often as admiring parties happen to drop in upon them.

While the lion was exhibiting in this way, his keeper was not idle, for he mingled among the crowd, and spread his praises most industriously. To one gentleman he whispered some very choice thing that the noble animal had said in the very act of coming up stairs, which, of course, rendered the mental effort still more astonishing; to another he murmured a hasty account of a grand dinner that had taken place the day before, where twenty-seven gentlemen had got up all at once to demand an extra cheer for the lion; and to the ladies he made sundry promises of interceding to procure the majestic brute's sign-manual for their albums. Then, there were little private consultations in different corners, relative to the personal appearance and stature of the lion; whether he was shorter than they had expected to see him, or taller, or thinner, or fatter, or younger, or older; whether he was like his portrait, or unlike it; and whether the particular shade of his eyes was black, or blue, or hazel, or green, or yellow, or mixture. At all these consultations the keeper assisted; and, in short, the lion was the sole and single subject of discussion till they sat him down to whist, and then the people relapsed into their old topics of conversation – themselves and each other.

We must confess that we looked forward with no slight impatience to the announcement of supper; for if you wish to see a tame lion under particularly favourable circumstances, feeding-time is the period of all others to pitch upon. We were therefore very much delighted to observe a sensation among the guests, which we well knew how to interpret, and immediately afterwards to behold the lion escorting the lady of the house downstairs. We offered our arm to an elderly female of our acquaintance, who – dear old soul! – is the very best person that ever lived, to lead down to any meal; for, be the room ever so small, or the party ever so large, she is sure, by some intuitive perception of the eligible, to push and pull herself and conductor close to the best dishes on the table; –

we say we offered our arm to this elderly female, and, descending the stairs shortly after the lion, were fortunate enough to obtain a seat nearly opposite him.

Of course the keeper was there already. He had planted himself at precisely that distance from his charge which afforded him a decent pretext for raising his voice, when he addressed him, to so loud a key, as could not fail to attract the attention of the whole company, and immediately began to apply himself seriously to the task of bringing the lion out, and putting him through the whole of his manoeuvres. Such flashes of wit as he elicited from the lion! First of all, they began to make puns upon a salt-cellar, and then upon the breast of a fowl, and then upon the trifle; but the best jokes of all were decidedly on the lobster salad, upon which latter subject the lion came out most vigorously, and, in the opinion of the most competent authorities, quite outshone himself. This is a very excellent mode of shining in society, and is founded, we humbly conceive, upon the classic model of the dialogues between Mr. Punch and his friend the proprietor, wherein the latter takes all the uphill work, and is content to pioneer to the jokes and repartees of Mr. P. himself, who never fails to gain great credit and excite much laughter thereby. Whatever it be founded on, however, we recommend it to all lions, present and to come; for in this instance it succeeded to admiration, and perfectly dazzled the whole body of hearers.

When the salt-cellar, and the fowl's breast, and the trifle, and the lobster salad were all exhausted, and could not afford standing room for another solitary witticism, the keeper performed that very dangerous feat which is still done with some of the caravan lions, although in one instance it terminated fatally, of putting his head in the animal's mouth, and placing himself entirely at its mercy. Boswell frequently presents a melancholy instance of the lamentable results of this achievement, and other keepers and jackals have been terribly lacerated for their daring. It is due to our lion to state, that he condescended to be trifled with, in the most gentle manner, and finally went home with the showman in a hack cab: perfectly peaceable, but slightly fuddled.

Being in a contemplative mood, we were led to make some reflections upon the character and conduct of this genus of lions as we walked homewards, and we were not long in arriving at the conclusion that our former impression in their favour was very much strengthened and confirmed by what we had recently seen. While the other lions receive company and compliments in a sullen, moody, not to say snarling manner, these appear flattered by the attentions that are paid them; while those conceal themselves to the utmost of their power from the vulgar gaze, these court the popular eye, and, unlike their brethren, whom nothing short of compulsion will move to exertion, are ever ready to display their acquirements to the wondering throng. We have known bears of undoubted ability who, when the expectations of a large audience have been wound up to the utmost pitch, have peremptorily refused to dance; well-taught monkeys, who have unaccountably objected to exhibit on the slack wire; and elephants of unquestioned genius, who have suddenly declined to turn the barrel-organ; but we never once knew or heard of a biped lion, literary or otherwise, – and we state it as a fact which is highly creditable to the whole species, – who, occasion offering, did not seize with avidity on any opportunity which was afforded him, of performing to his heart's content on the first violin.

MR. ROBERT BOLTON,
THE
'GENTLEMAN CONNECTED WITH THE PRESS'

In the parlour of the Green Dragon, a public-house in the immediate neighbourhood of Westminster Bridge, everybody talks politics, every evening, the great political authority being Mr. Robert Bolton, an individual who defines himself as 'a gentleman connected with the press,' which is a definition of peculiar indefiniteness. Mr. Robert Bolton's regular circle of admirers and listeners are an undertaker, a greengrocer, a hair-dresser, a baker, a large stomach surmounted by a man's head, and placed on the top of two particularly short legs, and a thin man in black, name, profession, and pursuit unknown, who always sits in the same position, always displays the same long, vacant face, and never opens his lips, surrounded as he is by most enthusiastic conversation, except to puff forth a volume of tobacco smoke, or give vent to a very snappy, loud, and shrill *hem!* The conversation sometimes turns upon literature, Mr. Bolton being a literary character, and always upon such news of the day as is exclusively possessed by that talented individual. I found myself (of course, accidentally) in the Green Dragon the other evening, and, being somewhat amused by the following conversation, preserved it.

'Can you lend me a ten pound note till Christmas?' inquired the hair-dresser of the stomach.

'Where's your security, Mr. Clip?'

'My stock in trade, – there's enough of it, I'm thinking, Mr. Thicknesse. Some fifty wigs, two poles, half-a-dozen head blocks, and a dead Bruin.'

'No, I won't, then,' growled out Thicknesse. 'I lends nothing on the security of the whigs or the Poles either. As for whigs, they're cheats; as for the Poles, they've got no cash. I never have nothing to do with blockheads, unless I can't awoid it (ironically), and a dead bear's about as much use to me as I could be to a dead bear.'

'Well, then' urged the other, 'there's a book as belonged to Pope, Byron's Poems, valued at forty pounds, because it's got Pope's identical scratch on the back; what do you think of that for security?'

'Well, to be sure!' cried the baker. 'But how d'ye mean, Mr. Clip?'

'Mean! why, that it's got the *hottergruff* of Pope.

"Steal not this book for fear of hangman's rope;
For it belongs to Alexander Pope."

All that's written on the inside of the binding of the book; so, as my son says, we're *bound* to believe it.'

'Well, sir,' observed the undertaker, deferentially, and in a half-whisper, leaning over the table, and knocking over the hair-dresser's grog as he spoke, 'that argument's very easy upset.'

'Perhaps, sir,' said Clip, a little flurried, 'you'll pay for the first upset afore you thinks of another.'

'Now,' said the undertaker, bowing amicably to the hair-dresser, 'I *think*, I says I *think* – you'll excuse me, Mr. Clip, I *think*, you see, that won't go down with the present company – unfortunately, my master had the honour of making the coffin of that ere Lord's housemaid, not no more nor twenty year ago. Don't think I'm proud on it, gentlemen; others might be; but I hate rank of any sort. I've no more respect for a Lord's footman than I have for any respectable tradesman in this room. I may say no more nor I have for Mr. Clip! (bowing). Therefore, that ere Lord must have been born long after Pope died. And it's a logical interference to defer, that they neither of them lived at the same time. So what I mean is this here, that Pope never had no book, never seed, felt, never smelt no book (triumphantly) as belonged to that ere Lord. And, gentlemen, when I consider how patiently you have 'eared the ideas what I have expressed, I feel bound, as the best way to reward you for the kindness you have exhibited, to sit down without saying anything more – partickler as I perceive a worthier visitor nor myself is just entered. I am not in the habit of paying compliments, gentlemen; when I do, therefore, I hope I strikes with double force.'

'Ah, Mr. Murgatroyd! What's all this about striking with double force?' said the object of the above remark, as he entered. 'I never excuse a man's getting into a rage during winter, even when he's seated so close to the fire as you are. It is very injudicious to put yourself into such a perspiration. What is the cause of this extreme physical and mental excitement, sir?'

Such was the very philosophical address of Mr. Robert Bolton, a shorthand-writer, as he termed himself – a bit of equivoque passing current among his fraternity, which must give the uninitiated a vast idea of the establishment of the ministerial organ, while to the initiated it signifies that no one paper can lay claim to the enjoyment of their services. Mr. Bolton was a young man, with a somewhat sickly and very dissipated expression of countenance. His habiliments were composed of an exquisite union of gentility, slovenliness, assumption, simplicity, *newness*, and old age. Half of him was dressed for the winter, the other half for the summer. His hat was of the the newest cut, the D'Orsay; his trousers had been white, but the inroads of mud and ink, etc, had given them a piebald appearance; round his throat he wore a very high black cravat, of the most tyrannical stiffness; while his *tout ensemble* was hidden beneath the enormous folds of an old brown poodle-collared great coat, which was closely buttoned up to the aforesaid cravat. His fingers peeped through the ends of his black kid gloves, and two of the toes of each foot took a similar view of society through the extremities of his high-lows. Sacred to the bare walls of his garret be the mysteries of his interior dress! He was a short, spare man, of a somewhat inferior deportment. Everybody seemed influenced by his entry into the room, and his salutation of each member partook of the patronizing. The hairdresser made way for him between himself and the stomach. A minute afterwards he had taken possession of his pint and pipe. A pause in the conversation took place. Everybody was waiting, anxious for his first observation.

'Horrid murder in Westminster this morning,' observed Mr. Bolton.

Everybody changed their positions. All eyes were fixed upon the man of paragraphs.

'A baker murdered his son by boiling him in a copper,' said Mr. Bolton.

'Good heavens!' exclaimed everybody, in simultaneous horror.

'Boiled him, gentlemen!' added Mr. Bolton, with the most effective emphasis; '*boiled* him!'

'And the particulars, Mr. B.,' inquired the hairdresser, 'the particulars?'

Mr. Bolton took a very long draught of porter, and some two or three dozen whiffs of tobacco, doubtless to instil into the commercial capacities of the company the superiority of a gentleman connected with the press, and then said –

'The man was a baker, gentlemen. (Every one looked at the baker present, who stared at Bolton.) His victim, being his son, also was necessarily the son of a baker. The wretched murderer had a wife, whom he was frequently in the habit, while in an intoxicated state, of kicking, pummelling, flinging mugs at, knocking down, and half-killing while in bed, by inserting in her mouth a considerable portion of a sheet or blanket.'

The speaker took another draught, everybody looked at everybody else, and exclaimed, 'Horrid!'

'It appears in evidence, gentlemen,' continued Mr. Bolton, 'that, on the evening of yesterday, Sawyer the baker came home in a reprehensible state of beer. Mrs. S., connubially considerate, carried him in that condition upstairs into his chamber, and consigned him to their mutual couch. In a minute or two she lay sleeping beside the man whom the morrow's dawn beheld a murderer! (Entire silence informed the reporter that his picture had attained the awful effect he desired.) The son came home about an hour afterwards, opened the door, and went up to bed. Scarcely (gentlemen, conceive his feelings of alarm), scarcely had he taken off his indescribables, when shrieks (to his experienced ear *maternal* shrieks) scared the silence of surrounding night. He put his indescribables on again, and ran downstairs. He opened the door of the parental bed-chamber. His father was dancing upon his mother. What must have been his feelings! In the agony of the minute he rushed at his male parent as he was about to plunge a knife into the side of his female. The mother shrieked. The father caught the son (who had wrested the knife from the paternal grasp) up in his arms, carried him downstairs, shoved him into a copper of boiling water among some linen, closed the lid, and jumped upon the top of it, in which position he was found with a ferocious countenance by the mother, who arrived in the melancholy wash-house just as he had so settled himself.

'"Where's my boy?" shrieked the mother.

'"In that copper, boiling," coolly replied the benign father.

'Struck by the awful intelligence, the mother rushed from the house, and alarmed the neighbourhood. The police entered a minute afterwards. The father, having bolted the wash-house door, had bolted himself. They dragged the lifeless body of the boiled baker from the cauldron, and, with a promptitude commendable in men of their station, they immediately carried it to the station-house. Subsequently, the baker was apprehended while seated on the top of a lamp-post in Parliament Street, lighting his pipe.'

The whole horrible ideality of the Mysteries of Udolpho, condensed into the pithy effect of a ten-line paragraph, could not possibly have so affected the narrator's auditory. Silence, the purest and most noble of all kinds of applause, bore ample testimony to the barbarity of the baker, as well as to Bolton's knack of narration; and it was only broken after some minutes had elapsed by interjectional expressions of the intense indignation of every man present. The baker wondered how a British baker could so disgrace himself and the highly honourable calling to which he belonged; and the others indulged in a variety of wonderments connected with the subject; among which not the least wonderment was that which was awakened by the genius and information of Mr. Robert Bolton, who, after a glowing eulogium on himself, and his unspeakable influence with the daily press, was proceeding, with a most solemn countenance, to hear the pros and cons of the Pope autograph question, when I took up my hat, and left.

SOME OTHER TITLES
AVAILABLE IN POCKET CLASSICS

*(A full list can be obtained from
Alan Sutton Publishing, 30 Brunswick Road,
Gloucester, GL1 1JJ)*

The Haunted Man and
The Haunted House

Charles Dickens

Everyone said he looked like a haunted
man. His was the voice of a haunted man;
slow speaking, deep and grave. He had the
manner of a haunted man. His lair was
solitary and vaultlike and anyone who saw
him in his inner chamber, part library and
part laboratory, on a winter's night before a
flickering fire, trembled.

Conversely, the narrator of the other
story first saw the haunted house in day-
light with the sun upon it. There was no
wind, no rain, no lightning, no thunder, no
awful or unwonted circumstance of any
kind, to heighten its effect.

And yet it was an avoided house, shunned by the villagers half a mile away.

Two of the best from the master of the
ghost story.

Lady Anna

Anthony Trollope

Lovel Grange was a small house, the residence of a rich nobleman, lying among the
mountains which separate Cumberland
from Westmorland, about ten miles from
Keswick. To it came Josephine Murray as a
beautiful young bride who considered it
quite the thing to be the wife of a lord.

She had not lived with the Earl six
months before he told her that the marriage
was no marriage – she was his mistress. Her
unborn child, the Lady Anna, could make
no claim to his title. Threats were issued by
the Murray family, a duel was fought, but
years of suffering were still to come. The
stage was set for high drama.

The West Indies and the Spanish Main

Anthony Trollope

In 1858 Anthony Trollope was selected for the job of reorganising the decrepit postal system in the West Indies. He was in London on November 1st making his preparations and by the 17th was outward bound for the Spanish Main.

The West Indian journey lasted until the following summer and besides the islands included extensive journeys in Central America and British Guiana. He began the book of his travels aboard a trading brig between Kingston, Jamaica and Cien Fuegos on the southern coast of Cuba and from then on the reader is treated to a racily humorous account of his doings in one of the most beautiful regions on earth.

The West Indies and the Spanish Main is full of personal anecdote and all the detail and colour of which Trollope was the master. Long unobtainable, it is sure to delight his many readers.

On Horseback through Asia Minor

Colonel Frederick Burnaby

(Author of *A Ride to Khiva*)

Armed with a single Henry Express rifle, a No. 12 smooth-bore, a small stock of medicines and a faithful servant, Burnaby set off in the winter of 1876/7 to ride 2,000 miles across Asia Minor.

War between Turkey and Russia was imminent, the whole area was a hotbed of intrigue and speculation, and reports of atrocities and massacres were widespread. His journey was to take five months and bring him into contact with Turks, Armenians, Greeks, Circassians, Kurds and Persians of all classes from pachas to farmers, from peasants to soldiers and nomads.

It was a ride of high adventure in wild, inhospitable country, through snow-drifts and over mountains, and Burnaby succeeds in sharing with his readers all the excitement, hardship and humour in this vivid account of Victorian travel.

Paris and the Parisians

Fanny Trollope

After the abortive attempt to open and run 'Trollope's Folly', her Cincinnati bazaar, Fanny Trollope returned to England to write *The Domestic Manners of the Americans* which brought overnight fame. But not consolation from her personal misfortunes – this was only achieved by travel and writing.

In 1836 appeared *Paris and the Parisians* which paralleled her earlier book in describing the domestic scene as it was in the French capital of 1835. Fanny was fifty-five with a gift for wit and satire and the ability to amuse some of her readers and infuriate others. With her pen she cut through the many layers of Parisian society to expose every facet of this glittering jewel. From her apartment in the rue de Provence she sallied forth on social and sightseeing expeditions. It was the Paris of Chateaubriand, George Sand and Franz Liszt, and Fanny Trollope brings it all to life.